FEAR THY NEIGHBOR

ETTIE SMITH AMISH MYSTERIES BOOK 18

SAMANTHA PRICE

CHAPTER 1

"I just don't know what to do."

Ettie looked up at her sister who was in her usual chair, knitting. "About what?"

Elsa-May looked over the top of her glasses. "You know what I'm talking about." Elsa-May's knitting dropped into her lap as she reached for a white handkerchief and managed to catch a sneeze.

"If I knew, I wouldn't have asked."

Tucking the handkerchief back under the edge of her sleeve, Elsa-May grunted. "I've created a problem in not collaborating with a certain person when I arranged to make teddies for the hospital."

"The bishop?"

"*Nee*, you know who." Elsa-May shook her head vigorously causing the loose skin around her neck to wobble.

"Ah. I know now."

Elsa-May had gone rogue and taken a group of ladies with her from the other knitting group in the community.

The other ladies were knitting for other causes including one of the children's hospitals. Now there was a rift among the knitters in their Amish community, which Elsa-May had been accused of creating.

Ettie pressed her lips into a thin line. "I don't know why everyone can't work together."

"That's what they were doing when I told the lady at the hospital I'd knit for her patients."

"You over-committed yourself."

Elsa-May leaned toward Ettie and jutted out her jaw. "And, it was your fault."

Ettie looked up from the sampler she was sewing. "How does everything end up my fault?"

"It was because of you I met the lady at the hospital."

"Me?"

Elsa-May nodded.

Ettie tried to recall how they met the head of the volunteers at the hospital some months back. They'd been asking the lady questions about a mystery, she was certain of that. "I can't remember exactly. It's all a bit fuzzy."

"That's always convenient for you not to remember things. I'd say your memory is selective."

"I've always been the same. I can always recall the important things so that wasn't important enough for me to remember. Anyway, you were the one who opened your mouth and flapped your gums. I didn't even know you were going to offer to make those teddy bears, and that was even before you stole the other ladies to help."

"What's done is done." Elsa-May grabbed her handkerchief just in time for another sneeze. This one was louder than the last, and it woke Snowy.

"It's all right Snowy, it wasn't an earthquake. It was just your *Mamm* sneezing."

Elsa-May chuckled. "*Mamm.* You're so silly, Ettie. I'm his owner."

"He doesn't know that." Ettie looked back at Snowy as he closed his eyes and placed his head back down on his furry pillow. It was okay for a dog to sleep all day, but Ettie didn't want another day being trapped inside the four walls because of Elsa-May's cold. Her sister resented her going anywhere without her while she was ill, so she was stuck there. Ettie frowned at her sister and then picked up her needlework.

"It seems like another lovely day outside."

"We wouldn't know, trapped in here." Ettie glanced out the window.

"I can see the blue skies from here."

It might as well be raining. In fact, Ettie would've preferred if it were. "When you're better, the first thing we'll do is visit Ava. We can't see her with you coughing and sneezing everywhere. She won't want your germs near the *boppli.* Come to think of it, we'll need to wash all those teddies in that bag over there before we send them to the hospital."

"Did you think I didn't think of that? Of course, we'll wash them and then hang them in the sun."

Ettie kept silent, shaking her head carefully so that Elsa-May wouldn't see her out of the corner of her eye. After several minutes of silence, Ettie's thoughts turned to their neighbors. "Have you noticed the Charmers are quieter than usual?"

Looking over the top of her glasses, Elsa-May said,

"That's where you're wrong. They've been quiet for some time, so that is the pattern of things now."

"Jah, but why so quiet all of a sudden after they've been complaining about Snowy, complaining about the fence, and everything else?"

"Greville's been in the hospital and obviously he's not well, so that's why. It doesn't take a genius to figure that out."

Ettie ignored her sister's jibes. "I know. He hasn't been to work for two weeks."

"Jah, well, you'd know, seeing you've been hanging out of the window spying on them ever since they moved in."

"I haven't." Ettie's mouth fell open at her sister's rudeness.

"Jah, you have, Ettie, and you can't deny it. You've even moved that chair close to the window so you can spy on them."

Ettie looked over at the wooden chair she'd positioned to get a better view. "It's to see the birds flying about in the trees out front, and to enjoy the scenery of the distant hills."

Elsa-May chuckled. "What about the pink and orange hues of the beautiful sunsets?"

"Jah, that too."

"Ha, got you there! The sun sets over the back of the *haus* and not the front."

Frowning, Ettie huffed, not liking to be caught out. "Well, I'm only checking on them because I don't trust them. What about how Stacey stole our mail?"

"She gave the letter back, so technically it wasn't stolen and she had an excuse for doing that."

"What about the mail she didn't give back? *Jah*, what about that?"

After another sneeze, Elsa-May groaned. "Oh, Ettie, there was never any mail she didn't give back. Why would she want to read any of our letters anyway? They're not interesting even to us."

Ettie thought back to their last interaction with Stacey Charmers. She'd told them Greville was in the hospital with … "Was it stomach problems he had?"

"I don't know. Don't you have that in your notes?"

"Notes?"

"*Jah*, the notes you're keeping on them." Another giggle escaped Elsa-May's lips and Ettie managed a chuckle.

"You're very funny, aren't you?"

"Not according to you. The Charmers are probably moving out because you've been spying on them and making them feel uncomfortable by always looking out the window at them like some kind of madwoman."

"The way the light hits the window, they wouldn't be able to see me looking at them. You can't see through the glass when you're outside. We can see out, but they can't see in. I keep telling you this."

"Hmm."

Ettie laid her sewing down and tapped a finger on her chin. "Maybe he's killed her and then he left in the middle of the night. Now, he's on the run. He could be in a faraway country by now before anyone has even found her. She could be lying there on the floor just hoping we'll stop by and help her as she gasps for air holding her throat. What if she's in the house now taking her last breath?"

"Ettie, you've such an imagination. You've always been like that."

"She's got no children and no friends, so who would find her? Will you come with me to peep in the window? Just the one at the front?"

"I'll do no such thing. Anyway, you said this morning that their car was in the driveway and that means they're home, doesn't it?"

"That's right. Don't you think it's strange that we haven't heard a thing from them?"

"*Nee.* It's good. Greville's unwell. Anyway, all he does when we see him is complain about something we've done or haven't done, or complain about Snowy."

Snowy lifted his head and looked at Elsa-May.

"He's heard you."

Elsa-May chortled when she looked over at her dog. Slowly, he abandoned his small pillow, pushing it aside with his head, and then put his head back down between his paws closing his eyes. "Anyway, there's an expression, *don't poke the bear. Let sleeping dogs lie.*"

"That's two expressions."

Elsa-May's lips turned upward at the corners, and Ettie guessed her sister was amused at her saying something that she would normally have said to Ettie. "There is no way I'm going over there. I'm not setting a foot on their land and you shouldn't either."

"I wouldn't worry if he wasn't so aggressive, but you've seen the way he is with her."

"You don't know what goes on behind closed doors, Ettie. She could be a monster to live with."

Ettie sighed and looked back at her needle-worked scripture sampler she was stitching. She was glad it wasn't a verse about patience as she'd about run out of it. There was no point talking to her sister. They rarely agreed on anything these days. "I only hope you're right."

"Just stop thinking about the Charmers. You've been obsessed with them ever since they moved here and it's not healthy. The scripture says to set your mind on things that are above, not earthly things."

"Okay. Although, it's hard to set my mind on heavenly things when I've never been to heaven, but I'll do my best to put the Charmers out of my mind."

"That's all I'm asking."

Ettie resisted the sudden urge to look out the window again, she'd never hear the end of it from Elsa-May if she'd done that just now. Elsa-May dropped her knitting, grabbed her handkerchief, and caught another sneeze. Snowy didn't flinch this time. It seemed he was getting used to the loud sudden noises.

After a quiet day at home having no one stopping by, Ettie and Elsa-May had an early night.

"Ettie!"

Ettie was in the middle of dreaming she was walking in the sun-drenched fields on the farm where she and her husband had raised their children. She half-opened her eyes annoyed with Elsa-May for waking her in the middle of such a beautiful dream. It had been the same the last two nights. Elsa-May had said she had heard scratching in the attic. "I told you to call Jeremiah about it. It's just a rat or a mouse or something. He'll catch it and block off the opening where the thing's getting in. *Gut nacht.*"

"*Nee,* it's not that this time. I heard a scream from next door."

CHAPTER 2

ETTIE OPENED one eye and saw her sister looming over her. "It's your imagination. We'll call him tomorrow and worry about it then." Ettie turned away from Elsa-May, and sank her head into her pillow once more, wishing she could slip back into that nice dream.

"Get up, Ettie. I think it was Stacey who screamed."

Ettie sat bolt upright. "Stacey? Stacey, from next door … screamed?"

"*Jah.*"

"Why didn't you say so?" Ettie flung the covers off, reached up and grabbed her dressing gown from its peg beside her bed. Swiftly, she swung her legs over the side of the bed and slipped her bare feet into her boots.

"What should we do?"

"I'm going over there." Ettie grabbed her white prayer *kapp* and pulled it on her head, noticing her clock read a little after eleven. "You said you heard a scream?"

"I'm sure it was."

"Let's go. I told you he'd kill her one day. I just knew it."

Elsa-May hurried into her room and came out dressed in her coat and pulling on her prayer *kapp*. "I'm ready."

"Shoes." Ettie said looking down at Elsa-May's bare feet.

"They're at the door."

Both ladies hurried over to the door and, after Elsa-May pulled on her boots, Ettie opened the door. Snowy was close behind them and Elsa-May pushed him back and closed him in the house. They crossed to the neighboring house, carefully because of the darkness, and knocked on the door. "Stacey!"

"I'm coming," Stacey called out. Then they heard footsteps, someone rushing about inside the house.

Ettie gasped. "She's alive." Then Ettie worried Greville would come to the door and yell at them for disturbing them in the middle of the night.

Stacey flung the door open and her face said everything. "He's dead. He's dead. Greville's dead." Her face screwed up and her eyes opened wide.

"What happened?" Elsa-May asked.

Ettie held her hand over her wildly pumping heart.

Stacey leaned over taking a few deep breaths. When she straightened, she said, "Masked men came in. They were robbing the place. Greville tried to stop them." She howled then, burying her face in her hands.

Ettie put her arm around her. "Have you called the police?"

"Yes. They're coming. And the ambulance," she managed to say through sobs.

"Are you sure he's dead?" Elsa-May asked.

"I think so. He's lying on the floor and won't move."

"You better check, Elsa-May," Ettie told her sister.

Elsa-May nodded. "Where is he?"

"This way." Stacey led the way and the two elderly sisters hurried along close behind.

"What about the men?" Elsa-May asked before they walked through the door.

"They ran out and drove off." Stacey stopped and looked at her. "Didn't you hear their car drive away?"

"Quick, he might still be alive," Ettie said. "Every second counts."

Stacey ran through to the living room where he lay on the floor. Elsa-May stooped over the body. "He's not breathing."

"Feel for a pulse," Ettie ordered. It was then that they heard sirens and Stacey ran back outside.

"I'll leave it for the paramedics," Elsa-May mumbled.

Ettie pushed Elsa-May out of the way. She picked up his wrist. "Nothing." Then she went to feel for a pulse at his neck. Ettie saw the neck tie wrapped tight around his throat and red marks on his skin, and she backed away. "Looks like he was strangled." She looked around and nothing in the room seemed out of place. Then she saw what looked like a pair of men's pajamas on the floor in the corner of the room. Looking back at Greville, she noticed he was wearing a suit, complete with socks and shiny black shoes.

When the paramedics rushed through the door, Ettie and Elsa-May stepped back while Stacey sobbed just inside the doorway. Another paramedic came in and moved them all into the sunroom closer to the front door.

"He's gone," Stacey said, as they waited.

"What were these robbers after?" Ettie asked her. "Do you have valuables?"

"They were just thieves. I don't know what they wanted. Money, or anything they could sell for money, I suppose. They didn't get anything. I've only got my rings that I wear and a small amount of cash that was in the bedroom." They heard another siren, and then Stacey walked closer to the door and looked out. "That'll be the police. They'll want to know what happened. Can you tell them you heard a car?" She looked back at Ettie and Elsa-May.

"I was asleep," Ettie said. "I didn't hear a thing until Elsa-May woke me."

"Me too. I heard a scream, and that's all."

"That was me," Stacey said.

Elsa-May nodded. "That's what I thought."

"Can't you tell them you heard a car, Elsa-May? I mean, you probably did if you heard me scream, but you just need to remember you heard it."

"I can't say it if I don't remember it," Elsa-May said.

"So, it's a possibility it happened and you just don't remember it?"

"Anything's possible," Ettie said, earning a glare from Elsa-May. "Well, that's what they say. They say—"

"Who's this 'they,' Ettie?" Elsa-May's voice boomed and Stacey shuddered.

"Please, my husband has just died."

"We're sorry," Ettie said. "She didn't mean to be so loud."

Elsa-May patted Stacey's shoulder.

The three ladies moved into the hallway and, over Stacey's shoulder, Ettie saw two uniformed police officers walking to the house.

"It would make things easier, that's all," Stacey whispered. "It would make it easier if you could only remember you heard that car, Elsa-May."

"I didn't."

"Forget it." Now, Stacey was angry rather than upset.

Stacey walked outside and Ettie and Elsa-May stayed behind her. Once Stacey had spoken a few words to the police, Ettie stepped forward.

"We're just the neighbors. We live next door."

"In that house." Elsa-May pointed.

One of the officers nodded. "We will need to talk with you because you were on the scene when we arrived," he told her.

"Okay, but we don't know anything," Ettie said. "We just came here now because we heard a scream."

He tipped his head toward his female partner. "Officer Larriby will look after you for the moment, Mrs. Charmers, and then the paramedics will want to take a look at you." He looked at Ettie, saying, "You two will need to be interviewed, here or at your house."

"We'll go home and wait," Elsa-May told him. "Will you be okay, Stacey?"

"I don't know. I think so."

Officer Larriby walked toward Stacey as Elsa-May

looped her arm through Ettie's. The sisters said a quick goodbye to Stacey and walked away.

"Do you think we should've stayed with her? She's got no one else." Ettie glanced back at Stacey's house.

"We can go back after the police have gone."

"Okay."

When they were halfway to the house, a car's headlights blinded them, then the car pulled up and the lights went off. Detective Kelly stepped out of the car.

"Well, well, well. I knew this address sounded familiar." He sauntered toward Ettie and Elsa-May.

CHAPTER 3

"THE MAN ... THE MAN NEXT DOOR," Elsa-May—who'd seemed calm until now—stammered, trying to give an explanation.

Ettie sucked in her lips. "Seems like he's dead."

"What were the two of you doing there, might I ask?"

"Elsa-May woke me after she heard Stacey screaming."

Elsa-May glared at Ettie. "One scream, Ettie. Not screaming."

Kelly blew out a deep breath and then stabbed a finger in the air pointing at them. "I'll be back to speak with you two. Maybe not tonight. I'll stop by tomorrow." He glanced at the next-door house. "I know you haven't always gotten along with these neighbors."

"Okay," Elsa-May said, pulling Ettie along with her. "We'll see you tomorrow."

When the sisters were at their front door, they stopped and looked back at Kelly who was now talking with Stacey just outside her house. "Do you think he thinks we did it, Elsa-May?"

"Don't be crazy. Of course, not." Elsa-May wiped her boots on the outside mat.

"Then why did he say we haven't always gotten along? What was the point of mentioning that?"

"He was making a statement. It's true—we haven't always gotten along with Greville or Stacey."

Ettie shook her head. "What a dreadful way for him to go. Killed by robbers."

"We'll wait until the police leave and we'll go back and stay with Stacey. She must be dreadfully upset."

"*Jah,* that's true. Okay, good idea." Ettie was impressed with her sister's compassion and wished she'd thought of staying there with Stacey. She'd been too busy trying to work out what had happened rather than thinking to feel empathy for Stacey. "It's so unexpected."

"I know. Wipe your feet," Elsa-May said as she stepped through the doorway.

"I already did," Ettie replied as she followed.

AFTER A FEW CUPS of hot tea, Elsa-May and Ettie walked out of their house to see Stacey's place flooded with onlookers, press and photographers. Kelly's car had gone and so had the officers who had first arrived on the scene. Only one police car remained.

"It's the newspapers, Ettie."

"That's dreadful. Why can't they leave people alone? It's still the middle of the night."

"I guess they have a job to do."

Ettie shook her head. "That's no excuse to harass people."

They looked on as they stood on their porch. There were two police officers keeping the crowd back from the house. "We can't go over there until they go," Elsa-May said. "They wouldn't let us in, I'd imagine."

"No, they wouldn't."

"We should've insisted on staying with poor Stacey."

"*Jah,* maybe." Ettie bit her lip imagining how Stacey would feel right at this moment. "Too late for that now. Seems like they're all waiting to see Stacey." Ettie pulled on Elsa-May's sleeve. "Why don't we go through the backyard?"

"What do you mean?"

"We'll take down a few fence palings and knock on her backdoor, or her side door. She must have one. Everyone has more than one door in their house."

"You're right, Ettie, and I remember there was a door in the sunroom. The room we … the only room we were allowed in after the police got there. The door was off to the back corner."

"Perfect."

They closed Snowy in the house. Ettie picked up a large metal hooked tool that Jeremiah had recently left behind and managed to use it to pull down three palings. Ettie slipped through nicely, but Elsa-May got stuck. From the other side of the fence, Ettie got Elsa-May to stand back while she gave another paling an almighty kick, dislodging it from the nails. With a four-paling gap, Elsa-May was able to get through.

"You'll have to nail these back up," Elsa-May said as soon as she was on the Charmers' side of the fence.

"I have hammer and nails in the *haus.*"

"Good."

They made their way around the side of the house to the sunroom door and Elsa-May knocked on it.

"Who is it?" Stacey asked.

"It's just us, from next door," Elsa-May said just loud enough for Stacey to hear.

Stacey opened the door wide to let them through. "He was dead. They've taken him away."

Elsa-May shook her head. "We're so sorry."

"Yes, we are. Do you have someone coming to stay with you?"

"I don't have anyone. I have no children." Stacey blinked rapidly looking like she was holding back tears.

"Is an officer with you?"

"Only one. There's only one staying in the house making sure I don't contaminate the scene."

"Would you like us to sit with you for a while?" Elsa-May asked.

"That would be nice."

While Stacey and Elsa-May sat, Ettie peeped around the corner to see a police officer standing in front of the room where Greville had been. There was yellow crime tape across the doorway.

When Ettie sat down with them, Stacey said, "They're coming back with a crime-scene team, the detective told me."

"What did the police say?" Ettie asked.

"They said there have been break-ins around here. At least two in the past couple of days. They broke the frame of the front door just like this one to get in." A tear trickled down her cheek, and she repeated what she'd told them. "The police will only let me in this room because they said the rest of the house is a crime scene. They asked me to leave for a day or two but I've got nowhere to go."

"Are you sure there's not someone you can call?" Ettie asked.

"There's only my sister. She lives an hour away and we haven't always gotten along."

"Have you called her?" Elsa-May asked.

"No."

Ettie suggested, "Why don't you call her and tell her what happened at least?"

Stacey nodded. "I'll call her first thing in the morning."

Elsa-May leaned over and patted Stacey on her shoulder. "It would be good if you could stay with her for a few days."

Stacey sighed. "There'll have to be a funeral and everything. You're right, Elsa-May, I'll ask her if I can stay."

Elsa-May nodded. "That's best. Call her now and let her know what happened, yes?"

"I don't want to bother her." Cautiously, Stacey picked up her cell phone from the center of the table. "Do you think I should?"

"Yes." Both sisters nodded for emphasis.

Looking down at her phone, she mumbled, "I'll send her a message and let her know what happened. That way, if she's asleep I won't wake her." Stacey pressed some buttons on her phone and then placed it down. "Why would they kill him?"

"Tell us exactly what happened," Ettie said. "What do you remember?"

"We were in bed, Greville heard noises and told me someone was in the house and to stay where I was. I begged him not to go out there. He never listened to me. Then I heard scuffling sounds, there was a thud and then I heard a car driving away. I ran out to the living room and saw my dear Greville on the floor, dead."

"Where did the tie come from?" Ettie asked.

"Tie?"

Elsa-May nodded. "He had a tie around his neck."

"I've got no idea what you're talking about and I don't know why you didn't hear that car."

"I was asleep," Ettie said. "Elsa-May woke me when she heard you scream."

"The police will question you. That's what he said. It's your friend, isn't it? I've seen him at your house on many occasions. Detective Keldron, he said his name was, or something like that."

Ettie chuckled. "That's Kelly not Keldron."

"Oh, he spoke quickly and I knew it started with a K. I had a school teacher once called Keldron and that's what I got mixed up."

"We do know that detective. He's not a friend though," Elsa-May was quick to point out.

Stacey leaned forward and placed a hand over Elsa-May's. "Can you say you heard a car, Elsa-May? Could you do me that favor?"

"No, because I didn't hear one." Elsa-May pulled her hand away and gave Stacey a little pat on her shoulder. "I was asleep when you screamed and that's what woke me. No matter how many times you ask me, I'm not going to say I heard something that I didn't."

Ettie asked, "Why would you want her to say that? What's so important about hearing a car?"

"I just want the police to believe me."

"Of course they will," Elsa-May said. "Why wouldn't they?"

"I don't know. I guess you're right." Stacey rubbed her head. "I'm just so upset I'm not thinking properly. I've never been good with authority figures, like the police, they scare me."

Elsa-May patted her shoulder. "Just say what happened and you'll be fine."

Stacey nodded.

Ettie suggested, "Why don't you spend the night with us? We've only got the couch, but you might feel better than staying here sitting in your sunroom and it seems like your sister is asleep since she hasn't called back."

"Would you mind?"

"That'll be fine," Elsa-May said. "We can tell that policeman in the next room where you'll be if you're needed for anything."

"Thank you. I'll just change into some clothes." When she walked out of the room, the policeman on duty wouldn't let her go back into her bedroom. "But that's where my clothes are," the sisters heard Stacey say.

"I'm sorry, ma'am. I can't let you go anywhere but that room where you were."

Ettie walked over to Stacey. "Just come as you are and we've got some lovely warm blankets over there for you. You'll feel better after a rest."

Stacey glared at the officer, and then said to Ettie,

"Thank you." She turned back to the officer and told him, "I'll just be next door."

The young officer nodded, seeming uninterested where she went as long as she didn't go where she wasn't supposed.

"What happens now?" Elsa-May asked him.

"I've just been told to stay here and make sure no one goes anywhere they shouldn't. The house is a crime scene."

The sisters ushered Stacey out of the house and through her backyard, through the broken fence and into their home.

CHAPTER 4

AFTER ONLY TWO HOURS SLEEP, Ettie woke with a start. The memories of what had happened at Stacey's house flooded through her mind. She always knew there was something odd about the Charmers and what happened to Greville was more than a home invasion resulting in his murder. Ettie was determined to get to the bottom of it and there was no time like the present. Too many things didn't add up.

Once she flung off her quilt, she got out of bed and changed into her day clothes. Carefully, she walked out of her room so the floorboards didn't creak, and she listened for sounds of anyone who might be awake.

The first thing Ettie noticed was Elsa-May's door was closed, and when she made her way into the living room, she saw Stacey sitting on a chair looking out the window. Stacey sat in exactly the same spot where Ettie had spent many an hour studying Stacey and Greville's movements. It was odd to see her neighbor now in that exact same spot.

Stacey looked around. "Morning, Ettie."

"Hello. What's happening out there?"

"There are so many people outside. They look like a lot of little ants and there are people standing around looking. I guess they live around here. You and Elsa-May are the only neighbors I've met since I've lived here. They all keep to themselves. A policeman came to the door and said I should be allowed back into my house this afternoon."

"Oh, I didn't hear a knock."

"He didn't. I saw him walking up to the door early this morning and I opened it before he knocked."

"Well, that explains that." Ettie walked forward and looked out the window over the top of Stacey's head just in time to see another car stop in front. A man holding a camera jumped out. "It's more of those reporters."

"I didn't think of that. It'll be in the paper. Oh, this is dreadful. Why can't people just leave me alone?"

"How are you feeling?" Ettie sat down on the couch nearby.

"Wretched and I can't believe all this is happening. It doesn't seem real. Greville's gone. He's gone."

Ettie was sorry for her. "It's a dreadful shock."

Stacey jumped up. "I'm going to tell all those people to leave me alone."

Ettie stretched out her hand. "I don't know if that's a good idea. That's what they want, a good story and to see someone upset. It's best to stay away from them."

"My sister should be coming soon, I hope. I told her in my message to come as soon as she could in the morning. I hope I can stay with her."

"Do you feel like something to eat?" Ettie asked. "Then you can call your sister again when you feel better if she's not here by then."

Stacey held her head. "I couldn't possibly eat."

Elsa-May walked out of her bedroom and must've overheard. "You have to keep your strength up, Stacey."

"Oh, Elsa-May, the newspaper's come to write a story." Stacey put her hand to her heart and a tear trickled down her cheek.

"You don't have to say anything to them. I'm sure the police would rather you didn't."

Stacey shook her head. "I don't want to say anything unless they can help me find the person responsible for hurting Greville."

Elsa-May stood between Ettie and Stacey. "Don't talk to them unless Detective Kelly thinks you should make an official statement of sorts."

"That sounds like a good idea." She looked back out the window. "Oh, that's her now, my sister. I should get to her before she gets close to that crowd and I'll explain what's happened."

"Come back with your sister and have something to eat with us," Elsa-May said.

"I can't eat, thanks anyway. If my sister will have me, I'll go and stay with her."

"Okay."

The sisters walked her to the door and once she was outside, they hurried to look out the window at what was unfolding. The crowd was staring at the house where the murder had happened as though someone was inside and would soon come out. No one was looking at Ettie and

25

Elsa-May's house next door to see who was coming and going.

Both Ettie and Elsa-May looked out the window at Stacey's sister stepping out of a late model white car. The woman was similar in appearance to Stacey and looked a little older.

"I do hope she can stay with her sister. She needs family around her at this time," Ettie said.

"I'm going to make pancakes. Want some?"

Ettie put her hand over her heart. "Oh, where's Snowy?"

"Still asleep, why?"

"The fence. I have to fix it. I'll do that right now." Ettie took the nails and hammer from the cupboard where they kept the tools and headed out to the backyard. In the dark, she'd managed to pull out four palings without harm to them or the rest of the fence. In no time, Ettie put enough nails in them to keep them solid and upright. When she stepped back, she noticed they were a little crooked, but she didn't mind. All that mattered was keeping Snowy contained in their yard. She headed back inside and replaced the hammer and the rest of the nails, hoping she'd never need them again—at least not for the fence.

"Wash your hands, Ettie," yelled Elsa-May from the kitchen.

"I will. Give me a chance, would you?" As Ettie walked to the bathroom, she was nearly knocked off her feet by Snowy heading out into the back yard.

"Ettie, do you want pancakes? You never answered me."

"*Jah,* of course."

"How many?"

"I don't know. You choose. Two, three or four." Ettie washed and dried her hands before she went to the kitchen where Elsa-May was singing a hymn.

"Ettie!" The shrill call came from Elsa-May causing Ettie to jump. "How many pancakes?"

"I'm right here. No need to yell."

Elsa-May swung around. "Oh, I thought you were still in the bathroom."

"No. I've been here waiting for breakfast. I already said I don't care how many."

"How many?"

Ettie gave up. "Three please."

"Coming up. Is Stacey coming back today?"

"I'm not sure because she didn't say. It seems tragedy has reunited the sisters." Ettie suddenly realized how hungry she was. "How long until they're ready?"

"Two minutes."

Ettie pushed herself to her feet. "I'll just see what's happening outside." Snowy rushed into the kitchen nearly knocking her off her feet again on her way to the window. "Watch that dog, Elsa-May. He's all wound up this morning."

"Don't mind her, Snowy," Ettie heard Elsa-May say just as she reached the window.

"Pancakes are ready! Pull yourself away from the spectacle and come back into the kitchen."

Ettie had a last look out the window at the crowd next door and noticed Stacey and her sister were sitting in the car.

Once Ettie sat down, Elsa-May asked, "What's happening out there?"

"Nothing, just the same, and that's all I saw because you ordered me to the kitchen. Where is the breakfast?"

"One more minute."

"I'll make the tea."

When the pancakes were done, Elsa-May placed a plate down for herself and one for her sister, then she slid the steaming pancakes onto their plates. "It's just awful."

"Denke for this," Ettie said. "It's horrible to think something like that happened so close to home."

"I haven't heard of any robberies happening around here. Surely we would've known. Someone would've said something to us. I talk to most people in the street as I'm walking Snowy. They would've mentioned something ... I would've thought."

"I agree, but Detective Kelly would know best what crimes happen around the area." Ettie poured maple syrup over her pancakes.

"Do you believe her?" Elsa-May took a sip of hot tea.

"Nee, do you?"

"Nee. That's not surprising. Something's not right, and I can't buy her story. Why would she ask me to pretend I heard a car?" Elsa-May shook her head.

"I thought that was odd too. Maybe she killed him," Ettie suggested.

"By strangling?" Elsa-May asked.

"Maybe not. He could've died some other way. There could've been a bullet hole we didn't see."

Elsa-May grimaced. "It looked like he'd been choked with that tie around his neck and he did look like he'd been strangled. Not that I've seen too much of that kind of thing. I'm not an expert by any means."

Ettie sighed and cut up another piece of pancake. "I wonder what the autopsy will reveal. She could've killed him to put an end to his brutality."

"Then why wouldn't she have just said so?"

"She'd be terrified. Scared of going to prison, going through court, and all the rest. It's easier to blame it on masked men who were supposedly robbing the place."

Elsa-May nodded. "I think you might be right. Only, no one said 'masked men,' did they? Shall we say something to Kelly?"

"*Nee.* We're only guessing."

"Okay, you're right. It's got nothing to do with us anyway," Elsa-May said.

"She did say it was masked men, now that I think back, but if she was in her bedroom how would she know if there was more than one, or that they were wearing masks or not?"

"Maybe she heard their voices or saw them running away."

Ettie nodded and made a mental note to ask Stacey if that was so.

"I figured out why his pajamas were on the floor."

Ettie stared at her sister. "Go on."

"He knew who it was and it was someone he was trying to impress. So, he quickly threw on a suit and tossed his pajamas to one side where they wouldn't be seen."

"I don't know about that. His suit would've been in his

bedroom closet, so surely he would've gotten dressed in there and discarded his previous clothing there."

"That's true." Elsa-May nodded. "I can't think of another reason."

"Also, it was odd that Stacey said they were in bed, but then—"

A knock sounded on their door interrupting Ettie.

"Who would that be?" Elsa-May asked.

"That's Kelly's knock." Ettie hurried to the door. "Hold the dog back, Elsa-May." Snowy was hot on Ettie's heels and Elsa-May barely managed to grab his collar before Ettie reached the door.

"Good morning, ladies." It was indeed Detective Kelly standing there smiling in a crumpled brown suit.

"You must never sleep," Elsa-May stood behind Ettie with Snowy in her arms struggling to get to Kelly.

It looks to me like he might have slept in that suit, Ettie thought.

"I'm used to it. My poor wife, however, is not. Not yet. Can I come in?"

"Sure you can." Ettie stepped back and knocked into Elsa-May, who huffed and poked her in the ribs.

"I'll put Snowy in my room."

"You do that, Elsa-May," Ettie said. "Come and take a seat, Detective."

When the three of them were seated, Kelly interlaced his hands and placed them in his lap. "What do you know about your neighbors?"

Ettie looked over at Elsa-May, wondering where to start. "There was always something funny about them."

He tipped his head to one side. "How so?"

"He was so aggressive to her, and he's been that way to us too."

He nodded looking thoughtful. "Yes, I was here on one or two of those occasions. What about Mrs. Charmers?"

"She opened our mail and then brought the letters to us," Elsa-May said. "That's why Ettie thinks she's strange."

"What do you know of their background? Where they came from and such."

"They said they moved here because they wanted to live in a quiet neighborhood."

"Yes, and he would never allow her to have friends visit her at the house. They have no children and she doesn't work outside the home and I believe he has some kind of job in an electronics company. Is that right, Elsa-May?"

"I believe so. In the back of my mind, I heard where he worked, but I can't remember now, not exactly."

"You're both wrong about his employment—his most recent employment, I mean. He's recently become a chef."

Ettie and Elsa-May looked at one another, in shock. "A chef?" Ettie asked.

"Like a cook?"

"That's right, Mrs. Lutz. He works at a pizza restaurant. He works the day shift."

Ettie tapped a finger on her chin. "Stacey never told us he was a chef. He doesn't even look like one."

"A pizza chef you said?" Elsa-May asked Kelly, still in disbelief.

"That's right."

Elsa-May shook her head. "Well, I never."

"Why does it shock you so much?"

"I thought I heard where he worked and it wasn't at a restaurant. And chefs, I thought, were younger. He looks too grim to be doing something fun all day such as making pizzas. I've always seen that as a happy person's job because cooking is creative." Elsa-May looked downward shaking her head.

A smile brightened Kelly's face. "That's what he does. It's an upmarket restaurant, a pizzeria in fact. It's not one of those belonging to a chain. He's also the manager and that might have created him some stress. That could explain his demeanor."

"Anyway, do you know what or who killed him?" Ettie asked.

"Not yet. They're doing the autopsy now. That brings me to Mrs. Charmers. Does she seem like a stable person to you?"

Ettie pulled a face. She didn't want to cause the detective to be suspicious about Stacey, but the woman was weird and Ettie had always considered her to be that way. "It's hard to say."

"It seems he was strangled. That's the most obvious conclusion at this point," Kelly said. "I won't know for certain until I get the autopsy report."

"We couldn't help noticing that tie around his neck," Elsa-May said.

"And the marks," Ettie added.

Kelly nodded. "Have you seen any strangers lurking about the area in the last few days?"

Ettie and Elsa-May looked at one another. "No." Elsa-May shook her head. "And I'm out walking with Snowy every day."

Ettie leaned forward. "Have there been a lot of robberies in the area? We've heard of none."

"Not a lot, but there were two a few streets away in the last few days. Although, up until a week ago this was one of the quieter neighborhoods. I've only ever come here to speak with the two of you in the years I've been stationed here. That's why I'm wondering if it's not a robbery, but rather an intended, premeditated murder."

Ettie was happy to hear she and the detective were thinking along the same lines.

"And you think Stacey murdered Greville?" Elsa-May asked.

He shook a finger at her. "Don't put words in my mouth. I don't think anything at this stage until I get the autopsy report in my hands. I just wanted to get some intel from the two of you."

"Some what?" Ettie tilted her head to one side.

"Never mind." Kelly sighed. "Intel—intelligence, information, that kind of thing."

"I heard a scream and then Ettie and I went over there. When we got there, she'd already called the police, and ambulance and ..."

"And, Elsa-May checked him and he wasn't breathing."

"Ettie was just about to feel for a pulse in his neck when she saw the tie, and that's when we heard the ambulance. She had already felt for a pulse in his wrist and there wasn't one. They got here fast."

Slowly, Kelly nodded. "Did she say what was stolen from the house?"

"She said there was nothing missing. She hasn't noticed anything gone. None of their valuables were missing. She said she only had her rings and some cash that was in the bedroom."

Elsa-May cleared her throat. "It seems that they disturbed the robbers just in time."

"If there were any robbers." Kelly pushed out his lips.

"You think she killed him?" Elsa-May asked again.

Kelly opened his mouth to respond and Ettie cut across him. "You're wrong. He was the aggressive one." Ettie wasn't sure what had happened but she didn't like Kelly assuming someone was guilty at this early stage. It was best to keep an open mind until there was more information.

Kelly grinned. "We shall see."

"What are you thinking?" Ettie asked the detective.

"Time will tell. It's my job to suspect everyone close to the deceased until we find our man ... or woman." He stood. "I'll be in touch. Good day."

Both ladies stood and showed Kelly to the front door.

"That was a quick visit," Elsa-May said to Ettie once she'd closed the door.

"He sure was asking us a lot of questions. The police didn't come and ask questions like they said. Maybe Kelly told them he'd do it."

"That's only normal he'd ask questions, Ettie." Elsa-May sighed.

"Go back to bed, you look tired."

Elsa-May rubbed her eyes. "I'll be okay. I'll have an early night tonight."

Ettie walked over to the window and looked out. "Elsa-May, he's walking over to Stacey and her sister.

They're still out there. That's odd. I thought they would've left ages ago."

"What do you think he's saying?"

"I'm not sure, but it's times like these it would be good to have the ability to read lips. They're talking standing close to one another and glancing back at Stacey's house. It looks like they're cooking something up."

Elsa-May chuckled.

Ettie turned around and stared at her. "What's so funny?"

"You said, 'cooking something up,' and he was a chef."

Frowning at her sister's weird sense of humor, Ettie looked back out the window while Elsa-May sat down and reached for her knitting in the bag by her feet. "Oh, that was quick. Now he's leaving. He must've surely told her she was needed down at the station to be interrogated. I think he suspects her especially after what he said to us."

"Could be. Did you see those arms and shoulders on the sister, Ettie?"

"*Jah*, I did, why?"

"She's well-muscled. She'd have enough strength to strangle someone, even Greville."

"That's what I was thinking. Not about the sister, but about Stacey being too small to have the strength to choke him."

"*Jah*, you're right. She's far too small to have overpowered a big man like Greville. I always thought *he* might've killed *her*."

"You were wrong." Elsa-May looked over the top of

her glasses at Ettie and then Ettie looked back out the window.

"It was probably the sister who did it with those strong arms of hers." Thoughts whirled in Ettie's head at a million miles per minute. "What if someone knew he was violent with Stacey, and they went around there to reason with him and then things got heated?" Ettie looked back at Elsa-May in time to see her pained expression.

"In the middle of the night? No one wants to be reasoned with at that hour."

"Jah, of course you're right." Ettie looked back out at the crowd. There must've been around thirty people and many of them were taking photographs and still paying no mind to Stacey and her sister.

"I usually am right."

Ettie looked back at Elsa-May. "Well, what do *you* think happened, since you're so clever?"

"Just what she said."

"She wanted you to lie about hearing a car. A minute ago, you didn't believe her at all. Why the flip-flop in your thoughts?"

"She's scared and confused, that's all. Stop trying to make something out of nothing, Ettie. Isn't it traumatic enough that our neighbor was murdered?"

Elsa-May was the one making a fuss. Ettie tried to keep quiet, but then it got too much. "You said the sister did it with those muscled arms, and before that you said you didn't believe Stacey. You can't deny it. You said that about the sister only two minutes ago. Then you had that theory about the pajamas on the floor."

"That was wrong of me. I shouldn't have said such a thing. You're a bad influence on me."

Ettie groaned. No matter which way Elsa-May looked at things, it always ended up being Ettie's fault. To the click-clack of Elsa-May's metal knitting needles, Ettie pushed her annoyance aside and looked out the window once more. Once the crowd in front of the house dwindled to a few people, Ettie went into the kitchen to start the after-breakfast washing up.

CHAPTER 5

A LITTLE LATER THAT DAY, a knock on their door made both sisters jump. Ettie had been quite unprepared for visitors as she'd been talking with Elsa-May rather than looking out the window.

"Who's that?" Elsa-May asked.

"Answer it and find out."

Elsa-May walked to the door glaring at Ettie.

"It's hard to see from inside the *haus*," Ettie told her as she followed along behind.

"You're up now, so why did I need to get up?"

"You need the exercise. You shouldn't stay in one place for too long. Remember what your doctor said?"

Elsa-May hushed Ettie and then opened the door. Stacey was in front of them with her sister behind her.

"I'm going to Evelyn's house. She's been kind enough to write down her phone number and address for you in case Elsa-May remembers the thing she's forgotten."

"I thought you'd left already," Ettie said.

"We did and then I remembered I have hardly any food

in the house. I don't like a bare cupboard. My sister took me down to the store and now that there's no one outside my house, I can drop some shopping in."

Ettie thought it odd she'd think about food at such a distressing time, but maybe she was trying to stay grounded and be mindful of everyday things. While Stacey introduced the sisters to Evelyn, Ettie leaned across her sister and grabbed the piece of paper in Stacey's hand. "Thank you. And, do tell us when the funeral will be."

Evelyn stepped forward. "It'll be as soon as possible after they release the body. We're just waiting on that now."

"Oh, Evelyn, please don't call my husband 'the body.' It sounds so cold."

"I was just trying to let the ladies know he'll be buried as soon as we possibly can. And, you might have to lease your house rather than sell. It's always hard to sell a house where someone's been murdered. I think, by law, you have to tell people that these days."

"Where will I live if I sell?" Stacey asked.

"You can live with me until you sort yourself out."

"I don't need to be sorted out. No, I have a home right here. It makes no sense for me to move or to leave it. I'm happy here."

Ettie wondered why she'd be happy living in a place where her husband was murdered. How could she ever feel safe there again?

"No, Stacey. You can't stay here after what's happened in this dreadful neighborhood." Evelyn then looked at the sisters and gave an apologetic smile. "I didn't mean that the way it sounded. Your house is lovely."

"So is mine," Stacey said. "And I won't leave it."

"Let's think about that later. Right now, I need to get you away from this ... place."

Stacey looked over at the sisters. "Thanks for everything. You'll know where to find me in the meantime."

"Bye, Stacey," Ettie said.

"We'll see you soon, Stacey, and it was nice to meet you, Evelyn."

Evelyn shot Elsa-May a smile and then moved Stacey along toward her car. When Elsa-May closed the door, she looked at the paper in Ettie's hand. "Keep that in a safe place."

"I will. I'll put it right over here on the bureau. Right by where we keep our coins for phone calls."

"Good."

"Did you really think it was nice to meet Evelyn?"

Elsa-May grimaced. *"Nee,* she was a dreadful, rude woman and so bossy."

Typical older sister, Ettie thought. "Then why did you say it was nice to meet her?"

"It's just a regular thing that people say."

"When you say something you don't mean, it's called a lie."

"Nee, Ettie, it's being polite. You could take a lesson from that."

Ettie's mouth opened wide. "Do you think I'm rude?"

"I didn't say that. I'm going to let poor old Snowy out of the bedroom and then I'll make us another pot of hot tea before you repair that fence."

"It's done, remember? I did it while you were making the pancakes."

Elsa-May nodded and Ettie didn't say anything further because she was too annoyed with Elsa-May. Instead, she sat down on the chair by the window and looked out expecting to see Evelyn and Stacey driving away in the car. "She's coming back, Elsa-May."

Elsa-May looked up from opening her bedroom door to let Snowy out. "Who?"

"Stacey. She's coming back to our house." Ettie hurried over to the door and opened it.

"I didn't want to say in front of my sister, but would you help me find out who did this to Greville?"

Ettie gulped and didn't know what to say.

"How would we do that?" Elsa-May asked, over Ettie's shoulder.

"Well, I did ask the detective if he was a friend of yours and he said no."

Ettie and Elsa-May looked at each other, each knowing the other's thoughts. It was one thing for them to deny being a 'friend' of his, it was another thing entirely for him to deny a friendship.

"Go on," Elsa-May urged.

"I asked why he was visiting you so often and he said you help him sometimes with crimes that happen within the Amish community." She went on to explain, "Because Amish people are odd and keep to themselves." When Ettie and Elsa-May didn't comment, she added, "And that's why you can help him—because they talk to you."

"Odd, are we?" Elsa-May crossed her arms over her chest, and Ettie nudged her in the ribs.

Ettie looked at Stacey's sad face and wanted to help her, even though she didn't think they could. "That may be so, or not, but how would we help? Greville wasn't Amish and doesn't know any Amish people, from what you've said, so I don't see—"

A tear fell down Stacey's face before she wiped it away. "You won't help me?"

"We'd like to, but we don't know you or Greville that much. And we don't even know anyone who knew him," Elsa-May said. "Do you see why it would be difficult?"

"We would if we could."

Stacey looked from one sister to the other. "You two were my closest friends these past months since we've lived here. Won't you even try?"

Ettie grimaced, sorry for Stacey if that truly were the case. They'd never seen Stacey as even remotely close to being a friend. "We wouldn't know how or where to start."

"Do what you usually do with Amish people, only do it with normal people."

Ettie frowned at Stacey wondering if she knew that she was being insulting.

"Okay, we'll help," Elsa-May said. "As long as you don't want me to lie about anything, okay?"

Stacey's face brightened, while Ettie couldn't believe Elsa-May had agreed to help.

Stacey leaped forward and hugged Elsa-May and then Ettie. "I'll be in touch."

Elsa-May and Ettie stood there watching while Stacey headed back outside and got into the white car with her sister. When the car had zoomed away, Ettie turned to her older sister. "One word, Elsa-May. One word. Why?"

"What else could I do? She was desperate for our help. And, it's so sad she thinks we were her friends. My heart went out to her."

"She thinks we *are* her friends. She truly seems to have no one else, except for her sister." Ettie closed the door. "What about the police?"

"I don't know." Elsa-May headed to the kitchen.

"Well, what about all those dreadful things she said about Amish people?"

Elsa-May chuckled. "She has no idea she was being rude. She's just ignorant."

Ettie unclipped the dog door and Snowy rushed in, ran around in circles for a bit, and jumped on his dog bed. Then Ettie noticed they'd left the front door open. When she'd closed it, she headed over to Snowy. "You're a good boy, Snowy. You didn't even try to get out the front door when we had it open just now." He looked up and wagged his tail before dropping his head onto his front paws.

"Who are you talking to?" Elsa-May asked from the kitchen.

"Just Snowy."

Ettie sat and looked out at the last few people milling around outside the house next door. Would they get new neighbors now? If Stacey stayed on, would she be at their place a lot, pushing her way inside with one excuse after another?

"Tea's ready." Elsa-May placed a teacup and saucer on the table in front of the couch.

"*Denke.* Are you having one?"

"*Jah.* But I can only carry one cup at a time."

Ettie moved to the couch, wrapped her cold hands

around the teacup to warm them, and then sipped her hot tea. When her sister came back out and sat in her usual chair, Ettie thought more about Elsa-May offering to help. "How are we going to do this?"

"What?"

"Find out who killed Greville."

Elsa-May blinked rapidly. "Do what we normally do. We wait to see what the police find out and go from there."

"Hmmm. Seems a lazy approach."

"Don't forget we—"

"Elsa-May, we don't know anything about Greville, or his background, or who his friends are—were, I mean."

Elsa-May shrugged. "I don't think he had any friends, and we can find out the rest. We can do this."

Ettie shook her head.

"We can find out where he worked and go from there."

"I guess." Ettie slowly nodded.

"I fancy a pizza one night soon."

"Ah, I see why you said we'd help," said Ettie with a giggle. "It's all about the pizza. You're never this enthusiastic about anything to do with investigations."

Elsa-May chuckled. "You're wrong."

"I'm not so sure about that." Ettie took another sip of tea thinking of how much Elsa-May liked her food.

"The first thing we need to do is find out where he worked. Kelly said it wasn't a pizza chain restaurant, so we'll check in the phone book and ..."

"Why don't we call Stacey and ask her where he worked seeing that she asked for our help?"

Elsa-May chuckled. "I guess we could do that. See, it's not so hard, is it?"

Ettie grunted. "You call Stacey later and get the name of the restaurant. We'll start tomorrow. Right now, I need a quiet rest of the day followed by an early night to make up for all that's happened around here."

CHAPTER 6

THE VERY NEXT DAY, Elsa-May and Ettie stood outside Emilio's Family Pizzeria reading the signage on the window. "They're open for lunch. Good. I'm hungry," Ettie said.

"Of course they're open for lunch, silly. Don't you remember they said Greville worked the day shift? The day shift is …. well, the day shift."

"I was just saying I'm happy about that because I'm hungry. Do we have a plan of how to go about this?"

"*Nee.* We'll just see what happens."

Ettie walked through the wide doorway and Elsa-May followed close behind.

"Table for two?" a young woman asked.

Ettie smiled at her. "There's just the two of us, yes."

"Would you like to sit near the window?"

"My sister would love to sit where she can look out the window. That's a hobby of hers."

Ettie giggled and the young woman's smile increased.

"I'll seat you at number fifteen." Once they were sitting at the table, the young woman handed them menus.

Ettie read the woman's name tag pinned to her uniform. "Lauren, what would you recommend?"

"The seafood pizza is good. That's number five."

Elsa-May shook her head. "No, neither of us likes fish."

"It's not really fish it's prawns—"

Ettie interrupted her, "What about number three? Three cheeses with three different types of meat?"

"Yes, I'll have that one." Elsa-May grinned from ear-to-ear.

"I'll have the same." Ettie closed the menu pleased that they agreed on something.

"No, Ettie. You can't have the same as me. If we're having one each, get a different one so I can try yours and you can try mine."

Ettie frowned and opened the menu again. "It's such a difficult choice." Ettie looked up at Lauren. "Have you worked here long?"

"I started at ten."

"I mean, how long have you been working here?"

Lauren giggled. "I see. I've been here two years this coming Friday."

"Ah, that is a long time."

Elsa-May blurted out. "We knew Greville."

Ettie looked at her in surprise. She'd been leading up to that.

The waitress shook her head. "It's so sad. Everyone's shocked. All the staff wanted to close this place today and the new manager wouldn't let us. He said we'd close it the day of the funeral, not both days."

"Oh, I thought Greville was the manager."

"He was a chef, Ettie," Elsa-May told her.

"Actually, he was both."

"Who's the manager now?" Ettie asked.

The young waitress looked over at the kitchen. "See that man with the black hair?"

"Yes."

"That's him. Nate Bowen."

The man was middle-aged and had jet black hair poking out from under the sides of a white chef's cap. "He's a manager and the chef as well?"

"That's right. Just like Greville."

"And how would Greville have felt about him taking over his job?"

Lauren smiled. "He wouldn't be happy about that."

"Why's that?" Ettie asked.

"Nate was always telling him how to do things better. They were constantly at each other's throats. One night there was a big ..." She stopped herself. "I shouldn't be telling you this."

"Go on," Ettie urged. "We won't say a thing."

"One night when Greville had to work a double shift, after closing they got into a physical fight. That's why one worked days and the other worked the evenings."

"That's dreadful," Elsa-May said.

"Yes, I was scared I can tell you that." She looked at Ettie. "How about the number ten? It's the vegetarian option."

Ettie smiled. "That'll be fine. I like my vegetables." When the waitress left, Ettie and Elsa-May stared across the red and white checkered table at one another. "Well, what do you think of that?"

"Dreadful. Why would you choose the vegetarian? You can have that all to yourself."

"*Nee*, I mean about Greville having an enemy."

Elsa-May huffed. "A man like him would've had more than one enemy. We should put him on the list though, what was his name?"

"Don't you remember?"

"*Jah*, I was checking if you do."

"His name is Nate Bowen." Ettie touched the side of her head. "It's locked in here. They hated one another and now Nate has his job. But ... people don't kill over jobs, do they?" Ettie asked.

"I wouldn't know. I'm sure the detective will interview everyone here. We're probably wasting our time." Elsa-May leaned back in her chair.

"How can you say that? We're here at this lovely establishment eating food we didn't have to cook ourselves. And someone else gets to wash the dishes."

Elsa-May chuckled. "You're right. We'll just enjoy it while we can."

"You can enjoy eating all that cheese and meat. You know what the doctor said about you having too much fat?"

"I'm sure it's all low fat, low calorie and all that. No need to worry. A good portion of it is the pizza base anyway." Elsa-May leaned across the table, and whispered, "Should we talk to Nate?"

"Lauren made it sound like everyone here will go to

the funeral. We could talk to him there. That would be more natural—less forced than trying to speak with him here."

"You're right." Elsa-May nodded. "We'll do it at the funeral."

Ettie leaned forward. "Say that again?"

"I said we'll do it—"

"Nee, the other thing you said."

Elsa-May frowned. "I didn't say anything else."

"You did. You said I was right and I'd just like to hear it again."

"I meant, you might be right. We'll have to wait until the day of the funeral to see if you are actually right."

Ettie sighed and shook her head.

"Anyway, Kelly might have everything solved by then."

When the waitress placed their pizzas down on the table, Ettie asked her, "Was Greville a popular boss?"

She stood there looking a little shocked at the question. "Not really if I'm honest. He wasn't ... well, I mean, he was moody. He used to fire people all the time until the owner said he wasn't allowed to fire anyone else, he had to retrain them."

"The owner?"

"Yes. Greville's cousin."

Elsa-May leaned forward becoming more interested. "Where's he from?"

"It's a she. She's from around here. She owns a few businesses around town." She got closer to them, and said in a quiet voice, "She's very wealthy."

"What's her name?" Ettie asked.

"Evelyn Chairgrin."

Elsa-May and Ettie stared at one another. Evelyn was also the name of Stacey's sister.

CHAPTER 7

EVELYN WASN'T A COMMON NAME, and Ettie guessed Greville had been hiding the fact that Evelyn was his sister-in-law. Unless, Greville had married his cousin. "Are you sure that's his cousin?"

"Yes, cousin. That's what he said. We hardly ever see Evelyn in here except when she hands out bonuses at the Christmas party."

Ettie and Elsa-May kept quiet and when the waitress left, Ettie pulled off a slice of pizza and nibbled on it. Staring at the two pizzas, Ettie considered Elsa-May's did look the nicer since her own was full of olives and hot peppers and smothered in a tomato sauce, with hardly any cheese at all.

"Ettie, that would mean that Stacey is also his cousin."

"What if the waitress is wrong? Greville might prefer to have people think he's working for his cousin and not his sister-in-law."

"Jah, you might be r …. could be." With delight, Elsa-May bit into her three cheeses and three meats pizza.

"Elsa-May, this all makes sense. The sister-in-law killed him because of how he was abusing her sister, and he was creating problems at work. For all we know this man who's taken his place might be a whole lot better at his work than Greville."

Ettie pulled her mouth to one side. "It's a little extreme to kill the man. She could've asked him to leave and why would she get involved in her sister's marriage? The two of them weren't close. Stacey clearly said that."

"She'd get involved because even if the sisters weren't close, she wouldn't want Stacey to be abused. And she couldn't fire him without making an enemy out of her sister. According to Stacey, the relationship with her sister was already strained. Evelyn might've killed two birds with one stone in getting rid of him."

Ettie shook her head. "It's all a bit far-fetched. I wonder what Detective Kelly will make of all this. Are we going half-half with the pizzas?"

"*Nee*, I'm eating all this and having your leftovers. You never eat the whole thing."

"How about you give me a slice now?"

Elsa-May looked over at Ettie's and laughed. "I told you not to order that."

"By then it was too late."

Elsa-May broke off a large piece for Ettie.

WHEN ELSA-MAY and Ettie got home, the place next door was still deserted. There were no cars, no evidence technicians and neither were there any press or police. The tape across the front of the house was gone.

Once Elsa-May was inside with Snowy jumping up at her, she held onto her stomach. "I'm so full."

Ettie untied her over-bonnet and hung it on the peg by the door. "If you're sick it's your own fault. You ate all your pizza but for the one piece you gave me, plus half of mine. I don't see how anyone can eat a whole pizza let alone a pizza and a half."

Elsa-May loosened the strings of her apron. "It was so good and you know it's my favorite food and I seldom get to eat it."

"Well, I hope you enjoyed it."

"I did at the time." Elsa-May sat down in her chair and pulled Snowy onto her lap.

"Can I get you anything?"

"*Nee denke.* I'll just sit here for a while and wait until I recover."

"We'll only need a light dinner."

"*Ach,* don't talk about food."

Ettie giggled and sat herself down on the chair next to the window and gazed out. When she glanced over a few moments later, Elsa-May was asleep with her mouth wide open. It hadn't taken long.

Looking back out the window, Ettie cast her mind back to the night Greville had been killed. It was late, yet he'd been fully clothed and in a business suit. Unusual attire for a chef and strange to wear at that time of night. And, who wears shoes and socks in their own home? Wouldn't he have been in slippers and pajamas? Stacey was in her nightie, so they hadn't expected visitors. Unless, Greville had just come home. But, that was different from what Stacey had told them. Stacey said they were both asleep when she heard noises and Greville went out to investigate. That had to mean Greville had been sleeping in a suit and shoes, and that didn't make sense. Then there were the pajamas tossed in the corner of the room. And, how did it come about that he got strangled with a tie? Also, why would the robbers have bypassed every other house in the street to rob theirs?

When Ettie heard a noise, she looked out the window. "Elsa-May wake up; we have company."

Elsa-May straightened herself. "Who?"

"It's Michelle Graber."

"*Ach nee.* Not her. What does she want?"

Ettie shook her head. This was the woman whose toes Elsa-May had stepped on. "We'll soon find out."

"How about you tell her I'm asleep in bed?"

Ettie stood up. "You're not."

"I was asleep until you woke me up just now."

"You have to face her sooner or later."

Just as Ettie had her hand on the doorknob, she heard Elsa-May mutter, "I'd rather it be later."

Ettie flung the door open before Michelle knocked. "Michelle, it's lovely to see you."

"Is it? Is that what you really think, Ettie?"

"*Jah,* of course. Come inside."

Michelle hurried past her and stopped when she saw Elsa-May. "Hello."

"Nice to see you, Michelle."

"Take a seat, would you? How about a cup of tea?" Ettie asked.

Michelle sat down. "What I've got to say won't take long. No tea needed."

"Oh." Ettie hurried to sit down, glad she wasn't the sister in Michelle's line of fire.

Michelle licked her lips, took a deep breath and then stared at Elsa-May. "I suppose you know why I'm here?"

"I'm guessing to suggest a collaboration?"

"Nee! I discussed with you some months ago that I was organizing ladies to knit teddies for the children's hospital and you deliberately stole my idea and stole all my knitting ladies. Not all of them, but nearly all."

Elsa-May nodded. "You're right and I'm sorry."

Michelle sat there staring at Elsa-May in disbelief. "You admit it?"

"Jah, I do. It was an excellent idea and when Ettie and I happened to be sitting across from a lady who organized the volunteers at one of the big hospitals, it just came into my head. I didn't mean to steal your idea."

Ettie leaned forward. "It wasn't a children's hospital either."

"Why didn't you come to me?" Michelle said. "We could've all worked together instead of creating a division."

"I thought you might have been upset with me. Everyone knows how you like to organize things."

"I do, that's true and I'm good at it. I could've taken over all that if you'd come to me after you'd been to that hospital. With your advancing age, don't you think you need to slow down instead of taking on more projects?"

Elsa-May frowned. "Everyone has an advancing age because everyone is getting older, even you, Michelle."

Ettie felt the need for a change of subject. Elsa-May

disliked being told she had to do things differently because of her age. "How are all your *kinner*, Michelle?"

Michelle's face brightened. "The last one's at school now. I was hoping for more but *Gott* hasn't blessed me with more. It seems Thomas will be the last."

Ettie smiled. "How many is that now?"

"Eleven."

"However do you find the time to do what you do, and with Peter's folks living with you?"

Michelle covered her mouth and giggled. "My two older girls help out and so does Peter's *mudder*. We all help each other and that gives me time to organize the volunteers and help with the other things I'm involved in." The smile left her face. "That was, until most of my knitting ladies suddenly started working for Elsa-May." Now she was back to glaring at Elsa-May.

"I'm truly sorry about that. How about a collaboration? Ettie and I have found it hard to keep up with the demand, so this could be the answer."

Ettie leaned forward. "Elsa-May overpromised and under delivered."

"I did no such thing, Ettie. I never promised anything."

Ettie leaned back. "I didn't mean that you said the word promise, but you did verbally commit to something and couldn't quite manage to deliver the amount you 'said' you would by the time you led the woman to believe."

"Then why didn't you say I verbally committed instead of promised, and overcommitted, under promised, whatever it was, and all that rubbish?"

Ettie shrugged her shoulders. "Never mind. It was just

a saying I heard someone say one time and I liked it. I won't do it again."

"*Gut!*" Elsa-May nodded and her mouth formed a straight line.

Michelle said, "Anyway, maybe that is the best way for us all to help not only our own community, but the broader community. That's always been important to me."

Now Ettie knew Michelle was there to make peace. "What a great idea, isn't it, Elsa-May?"

Elsa-May stared at Michelle for a moment before she spoke. "With my advancing age, I was taking great delight in guiding the women, being in charge of something before *Gott* calls me home. I would like to be in an organizing role because this might be the last chance I have before I die—seeing I'm so old and feeble."

Ettie knew Elsa-May was being beastly, but Michelle thought she was being serious. "I totally understand, I'd feel the same if I were your age. I only hope *Gott* gives me the chance to live to so great an age."

Elsa-May frowned at her and then Ettie had to intervene again. "Great! Problem solved. You'll both run a single group of knitting volunteers and both of you will be equally in charge. Fifty fifty, agreed, Michelle?"

Michelle nodded. "Sure. If that's okay with Elsa-May."

Elsa-May also nodded, even if she was gazing at the rug covering the floorboards.

Ettie continued, "Great. Now, Michelle, you'll never guess what happened next door."

"What?"

"Oh, Ettie, you're such a gossip." Elsa-May shook her head.

"I thought she should know. Everyone will know soon."

"Did something happen at Stacey's *haus?*"

Ettie and Elsa-May looked at one another. "How do you know Stacey?" Elsa-May asked.

"I came here once looking for you, Elsa-May, when you stole my first knitting lady. Stacey was standing by your mailbox and we began a conversation. She asked a lot of questions about the both of you."

"Oh. What did she ask?" Elsa-May leaned forward.

"I can't remember now. It was some months back. Anyway, what happened?"

"Stacey's husband got murdered," Ettie told her.

Michelle covered her mouth and gasped. "That's awful."

"It was intruders who did it. Seems they were trying to rob the place."

Elsa-May leaned forward. "How about a hot cup of tea?"

Michelle nodded. "I'm going to need something after that dreadful news."

After they became friends with Michelle and had hot tea and cake, they worked out a time for a meeting of their ladies so they could combine the demands of both hospitals. Michelle had insisted it be held at Elsa-May and Ettie's house and when that was agreed, Michelle left their place much happier than when she arrived.

"I'm glad she's gone," Elsa-May said as she looked out the window at the horse and buggy making its way down the road.

"Don't be like that. We're all friends now."

"Maybe."

Ettie shook her head. "Don't be like that. If anyone's in the wrong, it's you. You know Michelle had that idea before you and you—"

"All right. You don't have to go on about it. I hear what you're saying, but what I didn't like was how she kept saying I was so old."

"You are."

"I might be but it doesn't stop me from doing anything."

Ettie smiled. "I know. It irritates me as well when people carry on about my age. I feel just the same inside as I did when I was twenty. They'll know how it feels when they get to our age. You can't let it bother you." When the scowl still hadn't left Elsa-May's face, Ettie suggested, "How about I clear up these dishes and I'll cook the dinner tonight?" A faint smile hinted around Elsa-May's lips as she nodded.

CHAPTER 8

THE SISTERS DECIDED to call Stacey the next day, and Stacey confirmed her sister was indeed Greville's boss. They thought it best not to mention the fact that Greville had told everyone at work that Evelyn was his cousin. Then Stacey told them she would see them face to face soon, that she had something important to tell them.

Ettie and Elsa-May walked back home from the shanty that housed the telephone. "It seems like Stacey and Evelyn stayed away from the restaurant. Evelyn gave them Christmas bonuses, so we know she saw her staff at Christmas, and it seems like not so much during the rest of the year."

Ettie looked down at Snowy who was happily scampering in front of them, straining on the leash. "You're thinking Stacey didn't go near the restaurant because otherwise people would've learned Evelyn was the sister-in-law?"

"*Jah.* A lie like that would only work if Stacey wasn't ever at the restaurant."

"Maybe Greville told Stacey he didn't want her there."

Elsa-May nodded. "With Evelyn being the owner and Greville the manager, I would've thought Stacey would've stopped by whenever she went into town."

"They only had one car, though, and he drove it to work." Ettie knew that very well, as the odd thing was they never kept their car in the garage, but parked it in the driveway. There was no second car. If there was, she would've seen it.

"Hmm, that might be why. I wonder what she wants to tell us. Was her sister there and she couldn't talk in front of her?" Elsa-May said.

"It seems so. That's my guess, anyway. We should find out more about Evelyn if we can."

WHEN THEY GOT HOME, they did some chores while they waited for Stacey.

A loud knock sounded on their door an hour later, and Elsa-May put Snowy out the back while Ettie answered the door. It was Stacey. "Come in and sit down."

Stacey took a deep breath and planted herself on the couch next to Ettie. "The detective thinks I did it, I'm sure."

"Why would he think that?" Ettie asked.

"I don't know. Maybe because he ... I had to take Greville to the hospital a few times with stomach problems. Maybe they think I was poisoning him."

"Someone poisoned him?" Elsa-May leaned forward.

"No!" Ettie gasped biting her knuckles.

Elsa-May's fingertips flew to her mouth. "What kind of poison was it, Stacey?"

"What? There's no poison, Elsa-May." Stacey sighed and shook her head.

"Why did you say poison then, Stacey?"

"I'm just worried that they'll think I did it because Greville spent some time in the hospital. There was no poison—although some of the results are still to come in."

"I see. I'm sorry. I didn't mean to upset you."

"That's all right. The reason I'm here is to tell you the funeral is on Tuesday at the West Grove Memorial Grounds."

"That's a crematorium, isn't it?" Elsa-May asked.

"That's right. That's what he wanted. He wanted to be cremated and his ashes scattered at one of the places we loved to visit."

Ettie wondered if Greville had wanted a cremation, or if Stacey was trying to cover up evidence before a more detailed autopsy could be performed. If he was found strangled, they wouldn't go looking for other possible causes of death. It puzzled Ettie why Stacey had mentioned poison.

"What time?" Elsa-May asked.

"Eleven in the morning. Can you both come?"

"Yes, we'll be there." Ettie nodded and forced a smile.

"I don't like to ask, but how have you been getting along trying to find his killer?" Stacey looked from one sister to the other.

Elsa-May shook her head. "Are you sure there were intruders in your home the night he died?"

"Now, hold on a minute," Ettie said. When her sister

and Stacey looked at her, she continued, "What were you saying about poison, Stacey?"

"It's just that Greville had stomach problems, and I feared it might have been some kind of poison. Don't worry, I'm just getting myself worked up over nothing, I'm sure. I shouldn't have even mentioned it."

Elsa-May repositioned herself in her chair. "Stacey, before Ettie interrupted me I asked if you were sure there were people in your house that night?"

"Now you sound like the detective. I need you both to believe me. There were intruders."

"They didn't take anything," Ettie said. "Or leave any trace whatsoever." She didn't know that for certain, but if the detective had found something significant, he would've let it slip.

"I can't help it if the robbers were good at what they do."

Elsa-May rubbed her nose with her white handkerchief. "I'm not sure I'd agree since they left empty handed. How many robbers were there?"

Stacey looked down at the floorboards. "I don't know."

"Didn't you see them?" Ettie asked.

She shook her head. "No."

"How do you know they were masked?"

"Oh dear." Stacey put her hand over her mouth. "The detective asked me the very same thing and I don't know why I said it. I didn't see anyone and I don't know how many there were. It was an impression—a picture I had in my head when I heard the struggle. I was too scared to leave my bedroom."

Elsa-May tucked her handkerchief back in her sleeve,

and then asked, "What makes you think there was more than one?"

"I thought there would have to be more than one to overpower Greville. It's just what made sense. He was a big man."

Ettie slowly nodded in agreement. "Who would gain from Greville's death? Is there anyone?"

Stacey was quiet for a moment, as she put a hand to her cheek "I don't know. We had no money to speak of, only the house. What happened yesterday when you went to Emilio's?"

Ettie was shocked that Stacey knew they'd been to Greville's place of work until she remembered that Stacey had given her the address of the restaurant. "Nothing much…"

"The food's so good." Elsa-May grinned.

Except for the vegetarian one, Ettie thought.

"Thank you. They were all Greville's recipes. He changed the menu when he started work there."

"Where did the name Emilio come from?" Elsa-May asked.

"My sister bought it with that name, so I can't tell you any more than that. Do you think someone from there killed him?"

Ettie shook her head. "We were just doing some background work. As we said before we know nothing about Greville. We're just trying to piece things together. Why, was there anyone at work he didn't get along with?" Ettie asked, knowing the answer, but not sure if Stacey knew about Nate Bowen.

"I don't know. He never said anything. He never talked

about his work at all. The only thing he mentioned was that he liked it so much better than his last job. I could tell he was happier and more settled there. Funny thing was, he never cooked at home in all the years we've been married. Then my sister buys the restaurant and he decided to try his hand at cooking."

"How did that come about? Were you both close with your sister at that time?" Elsa-May asked.

"We were. We had dinner at her house nearly every week. We fell out over Greville's salary. Greville was worried with earning next to nothing compared to his last job. Evelyn and I had harsh words about it, and then …"

"Did he have enemies at his previous employment?" Elsa-May asked.

"He doesn't get along … I mean, he didn't get along with a lot of people. It's hard to say if he had a particular enemy if that's what you're getting at."

"What does your sister think about the way he died?" Elsa-May asked.

"Not much."

"Are you all alone at her house?"

"What Ettie means is, does your sister have family?"

Stacey shifted in her chair. "She's divorced and, like me, she has no children. Do you feel like you're getting somewhere with finding out who killed him?"

Elsa-May shook her head. "Not yet. It's too early."

"We're still gathering the facts. What bothers me is that he … you said you were both going to sleep. No, I believe you said you were both in bed when you heard a noise. Was Greville in his pajamas?" Ettie tilted her head to one side, interested to hear Stacey's answer.

She rubbed her forehead. "I don't know. I went to sleep first, so I thought he was, but then I remember when the police came and Greville was lying on the floor, he was in a suit."

"Why would he be wearing a suit if he was a chef?" Elsa-May asked.

"He wears—he wore—a suit to work."

Ettie frowned at her. No chef she'd ever seen wore a suit. "Really?"

Stacey blinked rapidly. "Sometimes, he does under his chef's white uniform. Oh, I mean, sometimes he did. I still can't get used to him being gone."

Elsa-May's mouth turned down at the corners. "That sounds extraordinarily uncomfortable to wear a suit and then put a uniform on over it."

"He did things different from other people. He said, as the boss and the head chef, it made him feel like he was properly dressed for his role even though he was the only one who knew he was wearing that suit." Stacey's giggles rang through the air.

Ettie frowned at her, pretty certain she was making it up. "And in the kitchen, don't they have a certain kind of footwear they're supposed to wear? I mean, they'd be rushing about in the busy times and the shoes he wore when he died looked very expensive and totally unsuitable for cooking."

Stacey's eyebrows lowered. "He wouldn't have worn those ones while cooking. He would've had other ones, Ettie. I just wanted to sit down with you both and see if you'd made headway. Thank you for helping me. I'm just worried that the detective will think I killed him."

"Don't worry. Everything will be fine, I'm sure," Elsa-May said.

"Do you think so?" Stacey asked.

"Yes."

Stacey slowly nodded. "I'll stay another night at my sister's and then I will come home. I'd rather be home, but my sister has been so helpful. I feel I should stay on tonight at least." Stacey stood up.

"That's good. Family are there when you need them."

"Evelyn says I should talk with a lawyer." She moved toward the door.

Elsa-May pushed herself to her feet. "Then maybe you should."

"Did Detective Kelly say anything to you?" Stacey asked, looking from sister to sister.

"No, and he wouldn't," Ettie said. "He can't talk to us about an investigation."

Stacey glanced at her wristwatch. "Oh, look at the time. I've so much to do. Bye." Stacey hurried to the door and closed it behind her. Ettie and Elsa-May had both stood to walk out with her, but she'd run out before they'd had a chance.

"Now what do you think, Elsa-May?"

Elsa-May shook her head. "She's a strange one. Always was, always will be, I guess."

CHAPTER 9

LATE THAT AFTERNOON, Ettie and Elsa-May had another visit from Detective Kelly. Once he was seated, he began, "Greville had poison in his system. It seems he was slowly being poisoned with arsenic."

Both sisters gasped because Stacey had talked about poison.

Ettie said, "One thing puzzles me. How did they get the toxicity report back so quickly? Doesn't it normally take several days?"

"These results came from the hospital. His wife mentioned Greville had been sick, so I checked with the hospital."

"That's right. He'd been sick," Elsa-May said.

"Their tests showed he'd had arsenic poisoning. When the coroner was informed on the hospital findings, he tested Greville and, turns out, he didn't die from any poison."

Ettie frowned at him. "He didn't?"

Kelly slowly shook his head. "He died from strangulation. In fact, even though the hospital found Greville had poison in his system, the coroner found nothing of the kind."

"Ah. Someone strangled him with that tie around his neck obviously," Elsa-May said.

Ettie frowned as she tried to figure out the puzzle. "Did he have two people who wanted him dead, Detective?"

"It's possible."

"Maybe the person or persons who killed him thought he was taking too long to die so they helped him along?" Elsa-May shook her head at the thought.

Ettie looked over at Kelly. "Do you still suspect Stacey?"

"Mrs. Smith, I'm not ruling anything or anyone out at this stage. I'm only telling you this because Mrs. Charmers asked me to keep you both informed. She seems to think you can help in some way."

"She asked us to help," Ettie confirmed.

"Don't go doing anything stupid. We know this is a murder case now, and not a robbery gone wrong. Don't get in my way, and if you find out anything you must let me know." The two sisters remained silent. "I know you want to help a fellow human being, but you don't know these people other than from them living next door. I doubt you'll be any help to her whatsoever."

"Elsa-May told Stacey we'd help her."

"At any rate, that was before we found out his murder was premeditated." Kelly rubbed his forehead. "Would one of you mind making me a cup of coffee?"

"I don't mind a bit." Elsa-May pushed herself to her feet and headed to the kitchen.

"Are you okay?" Ettie asked him.

"I have a nasty headache coming on." He blew out a deep breath.

"That's no good. You probably haven't been sleeping lately."

A gruff noise came from the back of his throat. "I haven't had a good night's sleep since I made detective."

While her sister was busy with coffee-making, Ettie told him what they knew so far from their visit to the restaurant.

"Thank you, Mrs. Smith, but I already discovered he'd been telling everyone Evelyn Chairgrin was his cousin. It seems he didn't want people to think he only got the job because his sister-in-law was doing him a favor."

"But that's probably exactly how he got the job. He wasn't a trained chef. We found out he trained after he got the job and that would've made some people a little cranky with him. The man who was the original manager was demoted because of him. Imagine how he would've felt taking orders from someone who didn't know what he was doing."

"I know. I know all that you're saying."

Elsa-May walked out of the kitchen with a mug of coffee. "Here you are, just as you like it."

"Care for some cake as well?" Ettie asked.

Kelly smiled. "I wouldn't mind a little something."

"I have lemon cake with thick frosting."

"Perfect." he said to Elsa-May before he even took a sip of coffee.

While Elsa-May was getting his cake, Ettie thought how to get more information from him. "We do feel a duty toward Stacey, so we can't really keep out of things. I know you're not happy with the idea—"

"Look, Mrs. Smith, I have no control over what a private citizen does in their own time. Just don't get in my way, okay? That's all I'm asking."

"Okay."

Elsa-May set a plate of cake down on the table in front of Kelly. "Would you like some, Ettie?"

Ettie shook her head.

Elsa-May took a piece of cake back to her chair with her. "Well, who are our suspects?" she asked once she sat down.

"Our suspects?" Kelly stared at her.

"Yes. I thought it would be better if we all worked together sharing information."

Kelly shook his head. "I don't think so. I was just telling your sister to leave this to us, the trained professionals. If you must proceed down the track you've started on, you'll get no help from me."

"Detective Kelly said we must keep out of his way."

"Oh." Elsa-May bit into the cake, chewing thoughtfully. After she had swallowed, she asked, "Then, why are you here, Detective?"

"To let you know that the murder was premeditated. It wasn't a home invasion like we first thought. Someone was poisoning Greville and then he was strangled, so putting all that information together—"

"Then you must suspect Stacey."

He looked over at Ettie. "Must I?"

"Or someone from his work," Elsa-May added.

"If you happen to think of something or learn of something, anything at all, please let me know." He took another mouthful of coffee.

Ettie nodded. "We will."

When Kelly had finished his coffee and eaten two pieces of cake, he stood ready to leave. "The mystery of the whole thing is, why wasn't the poison in his system at the time of his death? According to the medical experts it should've been."

"Perhaps a mistake at the hospital?" Elsa-May asked.

"No. That's highly unlikely," Kelly said. "They took three separate test samples on three different occasions."

"Are you going to the funeral?" Ettie asked him.

"I am. I suppose you'll both be there?"

Ettie and Elsa-May nodded.

CHAPTER 10

ETTIE AND ELSA-MAY sat in the chapel of the cemetery and crematorium waiting for Greville Charmers' funeral service to begin. Bored because they had gotten there far too early, Ettie looked around the room. It was full of highly varnished honey-colored wood from the floors to the vaulted ceiling. Being constructed of dark wood, Greville's coffin seemed out of place as it sat on metal supports between the two white opened curtains.

"How do we know we're at the right funeral?"

"Because I'd say this is the only one on this morning. The coffin's here already." Ettie looked around. "Here's Stacey and some other people now." People appeared in two groups, one at the front door and one at the side doors.

"We should say hello to Stacey."

"Not right now. She looks lovely in that dark blue dress."

Elsa-May turned and stared. *"Jah,* she does. It's only a plain dress, but it's the way she wears it that makes it look good. And, she's not in those high heels that so many of the *Englisch* women favor. The flat shoes suit the dress so well."

Within a couple of minutes, the place was half full of people.

Elsa-May leaned closer to Ettie, and whispered, "Here's the minister now. This must be all the people who are coming."

Ettie was only half-listening to her sister as her eyes were fixed on the front of the room. "I'd much rather become worm food than be burned," Ettie whispered, as she stared at the coffin wondering how much it'd cost. It seemed a shame to burn a perfectly new coffin.

"What does it matter what happens? You won't feel a thing, you'll be dead."

Ettie's mouth turned down at the corners. "It's the thought of the thing that matters to me."

"Good for you that you'll be buried then. I'll see to it." Elsa-May said with a sharp nod. Ettie managed a smile. No Amish she knew of had been cremated. Her smile didn't last long because her sister elbowed her in the ribs. "Ettie, there's the waitress from the pizzeria."

Ettie looked over to where her sister pointed. "Let's say hello. There's a few minutes before it's due to start, I'd say, because barely anyone's taken their seats."

"Okay. You go first."

As they walked toward Lauren, she saw them and smiled. "Hi. You were in the restaurant last week, weren't you?"

"That's right," Ettie said.

"I didn't know you knew Greville that well."

"We were neighbors of his," Elsa-May said.

"Yes, we lived right next door to him and his lovely wife, Stacey."

"Oh."

Ettie looked around at the people coming through the door. "Is everyone from your work here?"

"Yes. I think they'll all be coming. We've closed the restaurant especially for this."

Ettie looked over at Stacey who was at the front of the room talking angrily to a young man. "Is that man over there, the one who's talking to Greville's wife, one of the restaurant workers?"

The girl looked over. "Oh no. That's Greville's son."

"Son?" Ettie and Elsa-May jointly asked.

"Yes."

"How do you know him?" Ettie asked.

"I don't." She moved closer to them. "Between you and me, he came in a couple of times asking Greville for money. I only know he's the son because someone overheard them speaking. Greville said he was through with him and told him to get lost. He said he wasn't giving him another dime. Then the son tipped over a whole box of knives and forks and they scattered all along the floor. Then he walked out."

The organ music started. "I guess we should take our seats," Elsa-May said.

Lauren smiled at them.

Ettie wasn't finished talking with Lauren just yet. "He has quite a temper, then—Greville's son?"

Lauren nodded. "Seems so. We better sit." Then she moved over to sit with other young people, while the sisters made their way back to the row where they'd previously been.

"They have a son. Did you hear that?" Ettie whispered.

"I sure did. Now be quiet until it's over. Then we'll ask around and see what we can find out about the son and why he was kept a secret." Once again, Elsa-May nudged Ettie in the ribs when she noticed Detective Kelly walk into the chapel. Ettie rubbed her side, absentmindedly wondering if there'd be a bruise there later, and watched as Kelly sat on the other side of the room.

When everyone was seated, the minister stood and said a prayer, and then he talked about Greville Charmers and what a good man he was. Unlike at other *Englischer* funerals they'd been to, no one else stood to say anything nice about Greville. The service was over in a matter of twenty minutes. After the minister said another prayer, he announced that there were refreshments served in the adjoining room. The minister walked away, music played, and white curtains closed around the coffin.

"That was quick," Ettie whispered.

"I thought so too."

Ettie and Elsa-May stayed seated until most of the people had headed to the other room. "We'll split up and find out what we can," Ettie whispered. "There's Evelyn, I'll talk to her." Ettie left Elsa-May at the doorway and headed over to Evelyn. "Hello, Evelyn."

Evelyn smiled at her. "Hello. You're one of the neighbors. Stacey introduced us."

"That's right. We met the other day. How's Stacey coping?"

"As well as she could be under these grisly circumstances."

Ettie glanced over at Stacey and saw she was talking again to the young man they'd just found out was Greville and Stacey's son. Just to confirm, she asked, "Do you know that man Stacey's speaking with?"

"That's her son."

"Oh. She told me she didn't have any children."

"They only have Logan and he's been a real disappointment. They wiped him from their lives."

"Is that so?"

"Yes. He left home when he was sixteen to study abroad on one of those student exchange programs and then he got in with a bad crowd."

"That's a shame. He looks quite good. I mean, he seems well dressed and presentable."

Evelyn lifted her head high. "They've disowned him. They might as well have not had any children."

"What's wrong with him?"

"What's right with him should be the question."

"You said he went on a student exchange program, so does that mean Greville and Stacey had a student living with them?"

"No. Greville wasn't too well at the time."

Ettie wondered how long he might've been poisoned. "Greville was ill?"

"I think it was the stresses of his job. Then he changed vocations. He was a chef recently, and had been doing quite well, Stacey says."

From her reply, it didn't seem like she wanted Ettie to know she owned the restaurant where Greville worked, but other people knew. "That's right and you own the restaurant where he worked, don't you?"

Evelyn scowled. "Who told you that?"

"Um, someone who was here today. I can't remember who, but all the staff is here. Is it true?"

"It is. I suggested he step in and manage the place and he did a good job and raised the takings by thirty percent. He did that while becoming a fully qualified chef. I was lucky to have him."

Ettie looked back over at Stacey and saw the young man walking away. "What is Stacey's son's name?"

"Logan."

"Ah, that's right. You did tell me."

"Excuse me, dear. There are some people I should see before they leave."

"Of course." Ettie watched Evelyn walk toward the group of people who worked at the restaurant.

Elsa-May hurried over to Ettie. "Why do you look so worried? Greville and Stacey's son?"

Ettie nodded. "That's right. How many times did she tell us they didn't have any children?"

"Many times."

"Well, there he is."

Elsa-May shook her head. "Tsk tsk. And, the thing is, Ettie, if they lied about that what else might they have lied about?"

"If you remember, it wasn't Greville who said that, was Stacey."

"Only because Greville was yelling at us every time he saw us."

"I know." Ettie nodded. "Did you find out anything?"

Elsa-May looked around them. "I did. I found out that the person who used to be the manager of the pizzeria before Greville came, hated him. They were enemies."

"We already know that." Ettie tugged on Elsa-May's sleeve. "And, he would've had access to him to poison him."

"Shh," Elsa-May said.

"I said it quietly."

"*Jah,* but we're at his funeral."

"Well, keep it in the back of your mind," Ettie said.

"I will."

Ettie looked around. "I wonder if one of these people killed him."

"Very likely. Let's split up again and we'll come back together and compare what we find out."

"Okay."

Elsa-May rushed off, and Ettie was about to go in the other direction when she caught Detective Kelly's eye. She nodded to him and he walked over.

"I thought you'd be here," he said.

"I told you we would. He's our neighbor, or was our neighbor."

He smiled at them. "I mentioned to Stacey you've been a certain amount of help to me from time to time when I've been investigating your Amish community."

Ettie frowned. "That sounds awful. You mean when you've been investigating cases connected with our community," Ettie corrected him.

He chuckled. "You've been spending too much time with your sister. You're beginning to sound just like her."

Ettie grimaced. "Really?"

83

He nodded.

"Did you find out why Greville wanted people to think his boss was his cousin?"

"I'd say to make a friendlier work environment."

Ettie shrugged her shoulders. "Hmm, I don't really see the difference. Wouldn't it be just the same favor no matter if the cousin or the sister-in-law gave you a job?"

"You're right. I don't think it's a big deal." Kelly shook his head. "I don't know anything about that. I think someone could've simply made an error. He worked for his sister-in-law and maybe someone got confused and thought Evelyn was his cousin. Did you manage to find out anything that I should know?"

"The man who used to be the manager of the restaurant didn't like him because Greville took his job. Now that man has got it back again."

Kelly pulled out a notebook out of his inner coat pocket and flipped through it. "That would be Nate Bowen. We talked about this the other day when I was at your house."

"That's him, Nate Bowen."

Kelly pushed his book back into his pocket.

"Oh, and another thing. Stacey and Gr ... well, Stacey told us on many occasions that she never had any children. Now we find out she has a son." Ettie looked around Kelly's left shoulder. "He's over at the table now fixing himself a cup of coffee."

Kelly turned and looked over at the help-yourself tea and coffee table. "Is that right?"

"Yes. Did you talk with him?"

"She also told me she only had a sister. She never mentioned a son."

"Don't you think that's odd?" Ettie peered into Kelly's face, delighted that she had information he didn't know.

"Extremely. I think I should say hello."

Before Ettie could say anything, Kelly marched toward Stacey's estranged son. On looking around the room, Ettie saw Nate Bowen by himself and wasted no time seizing the opportunity to speak with him. Before she got to him, someone else had walked up to him. It was Elsa-May. Ettie stayed nearby to listen in.

"Hello," Elsa-May said, as she looked out the same window as he.

He turned around. "Hello."

"You worked with Greville."

"That's right."

"I heard you weren't a fan of his, and neither was I."

CHAPTER 11

NATE BOWEN TURNED to face Elsa-May more squarely and made a gravelly sound from deep in his throat. "What did he do to you?"

Elsa-May shook her head. "I was his neighbor and there were too many incidents to name. From complaining about my poor little dog, to the fence …"

"He was ruining my life. I can't say I'm glad he's gone because I wouldn't wish murder on anyone, but it sure makes things easier for me."

"I don't know how anyone could work with him," Elsa-May said. "It must've been hard."

He shook his head. "You've got no idea. When he first started at the restaurant, he had these crazy ideas about doing functions. He was supposed to organize things but he was never around and I was the one who had to pick up all the loose ends. When I complained, he told me to do my job and shut up. He said all the staff should stop complaining. It was then I knew I wasn't the only one who disliked him with a passion. He wouldn't listen to any of the staff. In the end, he stopped the functions. We didn't have enough staff to do that and run the restaurant."

"It sounds like he had big ideas."

"Yeah, ideas he should've kept to himself. Then, he wanted to change where we were sourcing the food. I'd made friends out of all our suppliers when I was running the place and I knew we were getting the freshest ingredients at the best prices. He comes in like a bull at a gate and offends all the suppliers and then they refused to deal with us."

"Oh, what did the owner say?"

"She didn't want to know about it. As long as the place made money. That was all she cared about."

"And did it?"

"The place is deserted by day and at night when I'm in charge we're running at capacity, turning the tables over three and four times since we are open until midnight."

"I see. It must be very hard for you to work there."

"It's convenient. I only live two blocks away, but I am … well, I was looking for another job. Now I'm manager again and as long as I stay that way I'll be happy."

"Good for you."

"Yeah, thanks." He smiled for the first time since they'd been speaking.

"I went there with my sister the other day for pizza. I must say that I did like the food, as much as I didn't want to."

"You should come there at night. I make the best pizzas."

"We don't go out at night much, but I'll keep it in mind if we ever do."

Ettie noticed that Nate's hair was far too dark for his face and it accentuated some of his fine lines. It was also darker than his eyebrows. The man dyed his hair to look younger ... when in fact, it made him look older. Ettie wondered why no one told him.

"How long did you know Greville?" Nate asked Elsa-May.

"They moved into the house next door a few months ago."

"I feel sorry for you."

Elsa-May leaned in toward him. "It wasn't very pleasant."

"Oh yeah, I can imagine." He chuckled.

"He took an instant disliking to my poor little dog."

Nate smiled. "The brute of a man!"

"I know. At first, I thought that and the other things were just teething problems and they'd settle down and get used to the neighborhood, but ..."

"Complaining all the time, was he?"

Elsa-May chuckled. "A good part of the time, yes. Oh, listen to me. I shouldn't be complaining about the man at his funeral."

A wide smile appeared on Nate's face. "What better time?"

Ettie had listened into the whole thing and didn't think Elsa-May was finding out enough about Nate. "Oh, there you are, Elsa-May."

"Ettie, this man here used to work with Greville."

"It's nice to meet you." Ettie held out her hand and he shook it.

"I'm Nate Bowen."

"Ettie."

"Oh, sorry, I didn't introduce myself. I'm Elsa-May. Ettie and I live together."

"Ah, so you lived next to Greville too."

"That's right and speaking about Greville's house, I heard a whisper that they might have found some evidence there."

His eyebrows shot up. "Is that right?"

"Yes. I can't tell you more than that because that's all I know. I wouldn't be surprised if the police make an arrest soon."

"I hope so. No one deserves to be murdered like that. Not even him. Excuse me, will you ladies?"

"Of course."

The ladies stood together as he left and Ettie noticed he headed over to his employer, Evelyn.

"What evidence have they got?"

"Nothing. I was just seeing how he'd react and he went to her. Interesting."

Elsa-May sighed.

"What did you learn from him? You were talking to him long enough."

"I know you were hovering behind listening to every word. You already know I didn't find out anything useful. I might have, if you hadn't interrupted us."

"I only did that because you were getting nowhere. I heard you laughing and giggling with him. We're here to find the man's killer not make new friends."

Elsa-May adjusted Ettie's prayer *kapp* causing Ettie to slap her hands away. "Stop it."

"It was crooked."

"I don't care."

Elsa-May said, "I wasn't making him a friend. Although, he could've had some good pizza-making secrets."

"I doubt it. To make good pizzas you've got to have the right equipment and a pizza oven would take over our entire kitchen." Ettie stared at Elsa-May.

"Who should we talk to now?"

Ettie looked around the room. There were the people who worked at Emilio's Pizzeria in one area. In another group, some ladies were huddled around Stacey, and a man in a suit, possibly someone from the funeral home was over in a corner talking to the minister.

Elsa-May sneezed.

"You stay here and I'll see what those ladies are saying to Stacey."

"Wait a minute." Elsa-May looked around the room. "Where's Detective Kelly?"

Ettie couldn't see him anywhere. "He must've been called away."

"What did he say to you before he left?" No sooner had Elsa-May spoken than she started sneezing violently. Ettie had to walk with her outside. Gone was her chance of finding out more.

"Your cold has returned—and gotten worse, too." Ettie offered her a clean handkerchief.

"I know. Let's go home."

"You stay here where you won't spread your wretched

germs and I'll go back inside and have someone call us a taxi."

"Okay, I won't move."

"I'll say goodbye to Stacey for the both of us."

"Denke." Elsa-May sneezed.

Ettie located someone to call a taxi for them, and then she found Stacey. "Elsa-May and I are going home now, Stacey. She's got a dreadful cold coming back so I really should get her home out of the weather and away from everyone."

"Thank you for coming. I appreciate it."

"How are you?"

Stacey managed a smile. "I'm doing okay."

Ettie didn't ask her about her son. It wasn't the time or the place. "Stop by soon, okay?"

"I will. I'll be coming home soon. I wanted to come home before now, but my sister said I should stay with her longer."

"That's good. Elsa-May is already outside. I made her wait there because she kept sneezing."

Stacey smiled and nodded. "I'll see you later, then. Bye, Ettie."

Ettie hurried outside and found Elsa-May waiting in a taxi. She opened the back door and climbed in with her.

"What took you so long?" Elsa-May asked.

"I was saying goodbye to Stacey."

Elsa-May sneezed again as the taxi pulled away from the curb.

CHAPTER 12

THE MORNING after the funeral the sisters saw Stacey again. From the window, Ettie watched her take two bulging plastic bags from the car into her house. Two minutes later, Stacey locked her door and headed to their house.

She bustled through their door when the sisters opened it. "I want to tell you that you can stop helping find out who did it. I'm just about to turn myself in."

"What? What for?" Ettie opened her mouth in shock.

"I did it. I killed him."

"Sit down, Stacey," Elsa-May said calmly.

Stacey inhaled deeply and then walked to the couch and sat down. Ettie joined her. Elsa-May leaned down and grabbed Snowy, who had been about to charge at Stacey. He often got excited to see visitors.

Elsa-May said, "I'll just put him outside." Ettie and Stacey sat waiting for Elsa-May to return. When Elsa-May had sat down, she looked at Stacey and said, "Now, what's this nonsense about?"

Ettie was glad her sister was able to stay so calm with a self-confessed murderess in the house. Elsa-May corrected her every time she said "murderess," insisting that "murderer" was now the accepted form for a killer of either sex, but Ettie had decided she would still use the feminine version in her mind. It just sounded better, she believed. "You killed him?" Ettie blurted out, turning sideways on the couch so she could see Stacey's face.

"I did, but it was in self-defense. You saw how he was. He often hit me. You saw the bruises on me, didn't you? You heard him yelling? He was always so aggressive."

"So, you slowly poisoned him?" Ettie blurted out.

Stacey licked her lips. "I didn't know how much of the stuff it would take. I've never had to do anything like it before."

"You haven't told Detective Kelly yet?" Elsa-May asked.

"No, I haven't."

"Did you tell your sister?" Ettie asked.

"No. She'd only talk me out of turning myself in. It's the right thing to do. I came to ask the both of you to stop looking for who killed him because I did it."

"Okay," Ettie managed to utter.

"Do you want one of us to come with you to the station? I'm fighting this cold of mine, but Ettie could do it."

"No thank you. It's something I'll do alone."

Ettie felt dreadfully sorry for her. They sat there in silence for a moment before Elsa-May asked, "Is there anything we can do for you?"

"No. I'm fine. I'll get a lawyer and I might get off or

just stay in jail a few years. Everyone knew what he was like and what a temper he had. I don't know how I put up with him for so long."

"Well, we all do what we have to do. My husband would never remember to take off his boots when he walked into the house. I was forever cleaning up after him and I do hate dirt on the floor, or even dust."

Ettie stared at her sister in disbelief. "Elsa-May, that can hardly compare with what Stacey's been through."

Elsa-May leaned forward. "I'm talking every single day, Ettie. I'd have to say, 'Please take off your boots.' By that time, he'd have tracked dirt halfway through the house."

"How could he forget? You had a mudroom."

"I know. Even the boys remembered." Elsa-May shook her head.

"Did your husband ever yell at you?" Stacey asked.

"No. He was a gentle and quiet man. It was only his messy ways that bothered me. I mean, how could he forget something that I told him every day?"

"Then Ettie's right, it doesn't compare. And, I'm guessing he never hit you?"

"No."

"I thought you two might've noticed what I went through with him."

"We did. We noticed it was hard for you, but what could we have done?" Ettie asked.

"Nothing. There was nothing you or anyone else could've done. I was too scared to leave him, or even tell anyone how I felt. For a start, where would I have gone? I would've felt like a failure if I'd left him, lived with my sister and had people feel sorry for me. I didn't have any money either. It was not easy. I thought about leaving him many a time."

"Was it easier to kill him?" Elsa-May asked. "He was poisoned over a period of time, so you had to have thought it through."

"I did, and I thought that was the solution. I would get to keep the house and what little savings we had. Everyone feels sorry for a widow. I suppose they won't feel sorry for me when they find out I killed him." She stood up. "I don't know when I'll see you again."

"And, Stacey, are you saying you strangled him?" Ettie asked, knowing that it didn't seem feasible.

"That's right. I'd had enough of him and his bullying ways."

Elsa-May stood too. "If you're turning yourself in, I guess they'll arrest you and you'll go before a judge, and you'll most likely get bail."

"You think so?"

"Yes. And then there'll be a trial, but these things are never fast. It might be a year or two away."

"That long?"

Elsa-May nodded. "That's right. Maybe quicker if you're pleading guilty."

"We don't really know. The lawyer would be the best one to advise you."

Stacey sighed. "Well, thank you."

"I'll water your plants while you're away."

"No, Ettie. Truly, don't bother."

Ettie shook her head. "It's no trouble."

"No. I don't want anyone near the house. I want it left the way I left it and that includes the garden."

Ettie nodded. "Okay, if that's what you want."

"Thank you." Stacey walked to the door, and then she turned to face them. "I'm sorry I didn't tell you right away. I don't know how I thought I could get away with it."

"Why now, Stacey?"

"It was my conscience, Ettie. I couldn't live with the lie."

Elsa-May nodded. "Fair enough. Before you leave, I want to ask you something."

Stacey raised her eyebrows at Elsa-May. "Go right ahead."

"Your sister looks very fit, like she plays sport and I was wondering ..."

"She used to play tennis professionally when she was young. She still plays in the senior sports division at the elite level."

"Ah, I knew she was an athlete," Elsa-May said.

Stacey lifted her hand and waved to them. "Bye now."

"Goodbye, Stacey," said Ettie. "Are you sure you wouldn't like me to come with you?"

"No. This is something I must do myself."

The two sisters stayed by the door until Stacey got into her car and drove away.

"That was the last thing I expected." Elsa-May closed the door.

Ettie nodded. "Me too. I thought it was the sister, and maybe, just maybe it is."

"And I was leaning toward the son. Hmm. Wait, what do you mean by maybe it is?"

"Stacey could be protecting her sister, don't you think? Stacey doesn't have the strength in her small hands to have strangled Greville."

"Why would the sister want him dead? He ran her business and increased the profits, she said. Besides, she might not even have known what Stacey was going through. Remember how reluctant Stacey was to call her?" Elsa-May sat down in her chair.

Ettie gasped.

"What is it, Ettie?"

"I don't know if it's anything, but it crossed my mind a while ago that Stacey seemed to be setting Greville up for something by having us think he was abusive. We never saw him hit her ... and did we ever hear him yelling at her?"

"I don't think so, but he was plenty aggressive with us."

"Possibly that was only to protect his wife from what she reported were her ghastly neighbors. Remember how Greville said Snowy was barking and then we found out that it was Stacey who had said he was barking? Greville hadn't even been home, and he was just going by what Stacey said. Then there was the fence that had the palings pulled down. We thought Greville did it when he blamed Snowy, but perhaps it was Stacey. That way, we'd only see the aggressive side of him and we'd testify in the trial. Or she'd want us to testify on her behalf."

"Now you're saying that, Ettie, but you never said that before."

Ettie opened her mouth wide in shock. "I thought that just recently, when I was thinking back. Why would I say it before I'd even thought about it? It certainly makes sense, though, as a possibility. If she long-termed poisoned him—which she admitted—what was to stop her long-term plotting and making herself a cozy alibi or even two?"

Elsa-May shook her head. "All I know is that you kept saying he'd kill her. Over and over, that's what you said. When they were quiet next door you kept saying he'd killed her, and you wanted me to go look in their windows with you."

"*Jah*, I admit I was wrong about that. It seems like Stacey did it. It's so obvious and everything points to her. I don't believe her." Ettie shook her head. "Something's not right."

"Why would she confess if she didn't do it?"

"To know that, we need more information. Perhaps she *is* protecting her son. Even though she had disowned him, maybe she still has the mother's instincts to protect."

"Maybe you're right about that."

A smile spread across Ettie's face at her sister's words.

Elsa-May lifted her hands. "Now don't get excited. I said '*Maybe* you're right,' Ettie."

Ettie chuckled.

CHAPTER 13

THE NEXT MORNING, Ettie just happened to be looking out the window when she saw a car pull up outside the Charmers' house. Naturally, she had to keep looking to see who it was. Two men jumped out and one was holding a large black camera. It was the press. Instead of them going to Stacey's house as she had expected, they walked toward her and opened their front gate. Ettie jumped to her feet. *"Ach nee."*

"What is it?" Elsa-May asked looking up from her knitting.

Ettie made her way to the door. "It's reporters and they're coming here to our *haus.*"

"What do they want?"

"I don't know. I'll find out." She opened the door before they knocked. "Good morning."

"Yes, good morning," the man without the camera said, smiling.

"What can I do for you?"

"Are you aware of what happened next door?"

"Yes. Of course. Everyone in the whole street knows."

He nodded. "Stacey Charmers confessed to killing her husband. What kind of person was she?"

"I have nothing to say." Ettie went to close the door and the man put his hand on it and held it open.

"Your neighbor, Stacey Charmers, turned herself in for killing her husband. Would you like to make a comment on the TV? The videographer will be here in a few minutes."

"No! I would not. Good day." Ettie closed the door, and then they knocked again. She opened the door. "Yes?"

"Would you like to make a statement off camera?"

"No." She closed the door again.

"She's confessed, then," Elsa-May said from her chair.

"I'd say so." Ettie walked over to the window and stared at the reporter and the cameraman leaving.

"Come away from there, Ettie."

"They can't see me." The reporter got to the gate, turned and smiled at Ettie. When Ettie scowled, he lifted his hand and gave a flippant little wave. "Cheeky, man." Ettie stood up and closed the curtains.

"What happened?"

"Nothing."

Looking over the top of her glasses, Elsa-May said, "Something must've."

Ettie sat down on the couch closer to her sister. "I thought people couldn't see in, but that man saw me. He looked right at me."

Elsa-May chortled, lowering her knitting. "I've been telling you that for several months. People can see you spying on them."

Ettie's fingertips flew to her mouth. "That means Greville and Stacey might've seen me watching them."

"*Jah*, I told you so."

Ettie sighed and sat down on the couch, well away from the window. "Oh, well. That's too bad."

"Next time, you might listen to me."

Their eyes met when they both heard a horse and buggy. Ettie jumped up. "Just when I leave the place where I can see all the goings on." She pulled the curtain aside. "It's Ava."

Elsa-May moved her knitting off her lap. "We should've gone to see her. It would've been such an effort for her to come to us."

"It's a good thing your cold's better again." Ettie opened the door and Ava was standing there holding her six-month-old son, Aaron. "Ah, here he is. Hello, Ava." Ettie glanced at the reporter and saw him snooping around outside Stacey's house while the photographer was taking photos of the house.

"Hello," said Ava. "I decided this was a good morning for us to visit you two."

Elsa-May pushed Ettie aside and stretched out her hands toward her great grandson. Ava passed him over with a smile and then they all walked into the house.

"I heard something happened next door." Ava looked at Ettie since Elsa-May was busy with Aaron.

"*Jah*, let's all sit down and we'll tell you." Elsa-May was making faces at Aaron while she was speaking, trying to make him smile.

"Care for hot tea, Ava?" Ettie asked.

"*Nee denke.* I've only just eaten."

Ettie rubbed her head once they were seated. "I don't know where to start. You know our neighbors were always a little strange."

Ava smiled and nodded. "I remember."

Ettie told Ava the whole story from the beginning, from when she was awakened by Elsa-May in the middle of the night, to going next door and finding Greville lying there, to Stacey finally admitting she'd killed him.

"What do you think about all that?" Elsa-May asked, carefully leaning the baby against her shoulder and patting him on his back.

"It sounds confusing. Why wouldn't Stacey admit to it in the first instance and then she changes her story now?"

"There could be a number of reasons. She might have been too scared at first, and then she realized she couldn't get away with it. Besides that, it seemed clear no one believed her story that there were robbers."

"She hasn't been back home yet. Elsa-May thought Stacey would get bail, but she hasn't."

"Not yet, Ettie. She might have to wait awhile. I was expecting her to come home today, but she could be out by tomorrow."

"She might've gone to her sister's place," Ava said. "Didn't you say she was staying with her?"

"That's a point. Anyway, tell us about you, Ava. What have you been doing?" Elsa-May asked.

"Nothing much. I've just been home with Aaron most days."

"How's Jeremiah?"

"He's been busy with work. We hardly see him these days. He leaves early and comes home late. *Mamm* comes over a lot to help me with Aaron. It's nice to have the company of a grown-up."

"Is he too busy to come and look at the cause of the rustling in our roof?"

"He's never too busy for the two of you. What's happening in your roof?"

"It could be Elsa-May's imagination, but she's sure she can hear scratching sounds at night."

Elsa-May pouted at Ettie. "You've heard it too."

"*Nee*, I never have. I've only heard you tell me about it. It must wait until I'm asleep, whatever it is." Ettie tittered, wondering if it wasn't in Elsa-May's imagination.

Ava smiled at Elsa-May. "Don't worry. I'll let him know and he'll stop by and take a look."

"*Gut, denke.*" Elsa-May gave a nod.

"There's always something going on with you two."

Ettie rubbed her head. "It seems so."

"We long for a quiet life," Elsa-May said.

Ettie didn't want a boring life knitting, as her sister did. She liked to keep her brain active and have something exciting going on; it kept life interesting. "You might like things quiet, Elsa-May, but mysteries and unexpected happenings are like a dash of color on a cream or a white wall. Life is boring without them."

"Who'd want color on a white wall? It wouldn't be white then, would it?" Elsa-May chuckled.

"Well, a wall is brightened with a colourful scripture sampler. If life were all white walls wouldn't that be boring?"

"It would, Ettie," Ava agreed. "There's nothing worse than living the same day over and over again."

105

"I think we need to be grateful for every day *Gott* gives us."

Ettie nodded, not wanting to get into an argument with her older sister. She wasn't saying she wasn't grateful. "That's true."

"Don't you think so?" Elsa-May asked.

"I agree with you."

"Hmm. Well, that's the first time today."

"Now, don't you two start." Ava chuckled.

"Start what?" Elsa-May asked.

"Squabbling. You're like children sometimes."

Elsa-May's jaw dropped open. "Ettie and I get along fine." Elsa-May stared at Ettie. "Don't we?"

"We do. Just like honey and peanut butter."

Elsa-May's mouth turned down at the corners. "Couldn't you have expressed yourself better than that?"

Ettie giggled. "Have you tried honey and peanut butter?"

"I wouldn't want to. Are you saying it's good or bad?"

Ava interrupted them. "I might take you up on that cup of tea, Ettie."

"Coming right up." Ettie pushed herself up from the couch and headed into the kitchen. She'd let Elsa-May ponder on that one.

CHAPTER 14

A MEETING of the two knitting groups had been arranged. It was unavoidable even though that's the last thing the sisters felt like doing when they had Greville's murder on their minds. At the end of the three-hour event, the groups had been merged and every woman had been assigned her knitting projects, and peace had been further restored between Michelle and Elsa-May.

Michelle was the last to leave, and as Ettie walked her to the door, she took the opportunity to ask more about Stacey. "Michelle, did Stacey, our neighbor, say anything else to you when you met her that day?"

"Hmm." Michelle's gaze turned upward to the ceiling. *"Jah,* she did. She talked about life and whether *Gott* punishes. She asked me what I thought."

"And what did you say?"

"I told her He sifts the wheat from the chaff."

"Did she say why she was asking?"

Michelle shook her head. "Not that I remember. Do

you think it has something to do with her husband's murder?"

"I don't think so. I was just curious, that's all."

THAT NIGHT as the sisters were going to bed, Ettie went into their kitchen and put out the light. She was in the process of pulling down the blind over the sink when a flicker of light caught her eye. She squinted then, and was sure there was a light emanating out of one of the windows in Stacey's house. "Elsa-May, what's that?"

Elsa-May took two steps in the dark to stand next to her. "That's someone with a flashlight inside the Charmers' house. I can see that even without my glasses."

"Who would it be? If Stacey was home, she'd just turn on the lights. She's not home—her car's not there."

"She'd still be in jail, arrested, since she'd turned herself in. Who is it? And why are they there?" Elsa-May peered out the window.

Ettie pulled her mouth to one side. "They might be looking for a clue to the murder, something hidden within the house. The police would come in daylight. And if not, they'd have no reason to avoid turning on a light. It's not them. What should we do?"

Elsa-May shook her head. "I don't know. We could run down to the phone in the shanty and call Kelly."

"Elsa-May, neither of us can run."

"That's true. What was I thinking? We'll have to see who it is for ourselves. You were always suggesting that I go over and peep in their windows with you; now I say yes. Let's go."

Ettie shook her head. Now was the worst time to do anything like that. "That was only when I *thought* he'd killed her, not now that there might actually be a murderer in the house. I haven't survived this long only to be killed. I was hoping to die in my sleep."

"Stop complaining, Ettie. Are you coming with me or not?"

"Nee and you shouldn't go either."

"I'm going." She looked down at herself. "Just as well I'm still in my day clothes. We've got to find out what's happening over there and how else are we going to know? We'll regret it if we let this opportunity pass. I'd reckon it's the person Stacey's protecting and when they go they'll be gone and we'll never know who it was."

Ettie pulled on Elsa-May's sleeve. "It's safer if we don't."

"We might be able to save Stacey from going to jail if she didn't do it." Elsa-May stared at Ettie. "I'll go by myself. Keep the lights off, so we don't alert them that we've seen them."

"Okay."

"Come along, would you?"

"Nee. I'll stay here. It's too dangerous."

"Suit yourself. I'll go alone." Elsa-May set off out the door and then a few seconds later, Ettie changed her mind. She couldn't let her sister go alone, so she followed her as quietly as she could. Just as Elsa-May had her hand outstretched to open their gate, Ettie tapped Elsa-May on the shoulder. Elsa-May jumped and then swung around. "Are you trying to give me a heart attack?"

"Shh. I decided to come with you," Ettie whispered.

Elsa-May put her hand over her heart. "Follow close, then."

As they shuffled in the pitch blackness toward their neighbor's house, through one of the windows of Stacey's house they saw another flicker of light. They were just past the fence line when they heard the Charmers' front door squeak open. Ettie pulled Elsa-May back and they crouched down and knelt behind the bushes that separated the front of the Charmers' property from theirs.

Quietly huddled on the ground, they saw a man run past them heading down the road. In the dark, Ettie had a fairly good look at him. He wore a hooded jacket with the hood pulled low to cover most of his face. He was tall, too tall to be a woman in men's clothing. When he was out of sight, they heard a car start. Ettie half stood and in the distance saw the headlights of the car as it moved away. Ettie stood fully and then helped Elsa-May to her feet.

"Did you recognize him?" Elsa-May asked.

"*Nee*, did you?"

"It could've been the son, but it was too dark to see."

Ettie took a deep breath to calm her nerves. "That's what I thought. He seemed young and agile by the speed at which he moved."

"Dash it all! I wish we'd got a better look at him and we might've if we'd been faster out of the *haus*."

"That's where you're wrong. We would've come face to face with him. We both might be lying dead right now if I we'd left the house a few seconds earlier. It's true we might have gotten a good look, but it would have been our last look this side of heaven."

Elsa-May started walking home. "We should call Kelly, and he could get the place fingerprinted."

Ettie shuddered. "I'm too scared to go to the shanty now to call him. That man might come back."

"It's just down the road, Ettie."

Ettie frowned at Elsa-May. "You go then."

"Not alone I won't."

"We'll go first thing in the morning."

"Okay," Elsa-May agreed.

Ettie stopped still and looked back at the Charmers' house. "Whoever it was must've known Stacey was in jail and not coming home."

"Many people would know that. Even the reporters knew she confessed to killing him. It wouldn't be hard to find out if she was still in jail." Elsa-May pushed their gate open. "If she is guilty, maybe she sent someone back to hide some evidence."

"That makes no sense. She confessed to it, so she wouldn't be worried about evidence. Anyway, she had plenty of time to hide things."

"Oh, that's true. Then I don't know what to think." Elsa-May pushed on their front door and turned back to Ettie. "Did you leave the door unlocked?"

"*Jah*, we always do."

"Not anymore we don't. From now on, we lock it. All right?"

"Okay, suits me fine. But then we'll have to remember to carry the key with us."

Once they were inside the house, they double checked all the doors and windows to make sure they were locked.

Then, too scared to sleep alone, Ettie slept in Elsa-May's bed until her sister's snoring became unbearable. In the early hours of the morning, Ettie forced herself to be brave and went back to her own room.

CHAPTER 15

ETTIE ONLY HAD a light sleep and was glad when the morning light streamed through her window. She changed into her clothes, then walked into the kitchen. Elsa-May was nowhere about, so Ettie put the teakettle on the stove and sat down to wait for Elsa-May to wake. Just as she was in the middle of brewing her first pot of hot tea for the day, Elsa-May staggered into the kitchen yawning with Snowy close by her side.

"Did you sleep well?" Ettie asked, remembering Elsa-May's snoring blitz.

"I didn't sleep a wink. How about you?"

A giggle escaped Ettie's lips. "I tried to sleep but you wouldn't stop snoring. I ended up going back to my room."

Elsa-May frowned. "I was snoring?"

"Jah."

"Are you sure it wasn't Snowy? He snores a lot."

"He was snoring too, but not as loud as you."

Elsa-May raised her eyebrows. "I never knew I snored."

"That's because you're always asleep when you do it."

"I must've had some sleep then, but I don't feel like I have. It was such a shock, what happened last night. As soon as we have breakfast we'll phone Kelly and tell him what we saw."

"Agreed. I wonder what's happened to Stacey." Before Elsa-May could comment, Ettie spoke again. "The other brother wasn't at Greville's funeral. His younger brother who was said to be in college."

"That's true. Nothing much has been said about him. Kelly will be able to tell us."

"Hmm." Ettie poured Elsa-May a cup of tea. "He's not being very forthcoming these days." Ettie sliced bread for toast, and then popped some slices under the griller.

"Once we tell him what happened last night then we'll ask him about the younger brother. For all we know it could've been the younger brother there last night."

"Could've been any one." Ettie sat down and drank her tea while she waited for the toast to brown.

AFTER BREAKFAST, Elsa-May had just snapped the lead onto Snowy's collar before they headed to the phone down the road when a loud knock sounded on their door. Snowy jumped up onto his hind legs, bounded for one step, and then strained at the leash trying to get to the visitor.

"That's Kelly now by the way Snowy's carrying on. He saved us a walk." While Elsa-May unclipped the leash and put Snowy out the back, Ettie opened the door. Sure enough, it was Detective Kelly.

"Good morning, I have something to tell you," he said.

"Come in. We have something to tell you, too."

His eyebrows shot up, as he walked to the living room, just as Elsa-May hurried back to her chair.

"Sit down. Would you like some coffee?" Ettie asked.

"No thank you. I'm trying to cut down." He patted his stomach. "I've already had coffee and a doughnut this morning." Detective Kelly sat down on the chair opposite the couch and then looked at the two ladies. "What is it you have to tell me?"

Elsa-May cleared her throat. "There was someone in the house next door last night."

"It was late, about ten o'clock, and they had a flashlight," Ettie added.

"Did you get a look at him?" Kelly asked.

Ettie pushed out her lips. "It's funny how you assume it was a man."

His eyes grew wide. "It was a woman?"

"No." Ettie shook her head. "We're positive it was a man."

He clamped his lips together.

"Elsa-May made me go outside with her. He passed us and we had to hide in the bushes."

His mouth fell open in shock. "That could've been very dangerous. You shouldn't have gone outside."

"Do you think it was a reporter?" Elsa-May asked.

Ettie added, "We can't think who it could've been."

Kelly crossed one leg over the other. "Unless it was their son. Looking for something perhaps? If he wasn't getting along with them, he wouldn't want to ask if he'd left something at their house."

"Yes, the son. That could be right. We were just getting ready to call you because we were too scared to do it last night in the dark. We thought you could send your team in to have a look around and take some fingerprints."

Slowly, he nodded. "We'll see. Are you sure now? You both saw this fellow?"

"We did!" Elsa-May insisted while Ettie nodded.

Ettie knew that every time Kelly said, 'we'll see,' it meant he probably wouldn't.

Elsa-May said, "Why have you come to see us today, Detective?"

"Oh, yes. You said you a reason for this visit," Ettie said.

"It seems Greville had an extensive stocks portfolio, and just a tad over three hundred thousand in life insurance."

"Dollars?" Ettie asked.

When Kelly nodded, Elsa-May gasped, and asked, "Do you think that's why she killed him?"

Ettie glared at her sister. "She said it was self-defence."

"Maybe and maybe not." Kelly continued, "Her story does sound less convincing now that we've found out about the substantial gains that were to be had from his death. It seems she was the sole beneficiary and nothing was mentioned about the son."

"What about Greville's younger brother?"

"We've talked to him. He distanced himself from his family some time back and wants nothing to do with any of them. And he had plenty of proof that he wasn't in this area at the time of the murder."

"Stacey said they had nothing else, but the house. Didn't she, Elsa-May?"

"That's right. She said they had a little savings and only the house."

Kelly shook his head. "Well, she was named as the sole beneficiary of the shares and the life insurance."

Ettie and Elsa-May looked at one another. "Where is Stacey now?" Ettie asked.

"She's confessed, been charged and she goes before a judge this morning and a determination will be made regarding bail."

"This morning?"

"That's right. Now, you say this fellow parked his car down the road?"

Ettie nodded.

He jumped to his feet. "Can you show me exactly where?"

"We can."

He pulled a phone out of his pocket. "I'll just make a call and get the team back here. Then you can show me where the car was. Hopefully, there are tire marks."

ONCE ETTIE and Elsa-May showed him where the car had been, they were pleased Kelly found tracks. Now they had evidence to prove they weren't making it up. He took photos with the camera on his iPhone in the interim. "I'll wait here until the team arrives, so they can work this area. Have you noticed another car here this morning?"

"No. No other car has been there," Ettie said. "I had a look out here while I was waiting for the toast to finish browning."

"Good, very good. Now, let me reiterate how important it is that you not put yourselves in danger like you did last night. Someone has been killed. Just be mindful of that."

"We'll be careful," Ettie said. "So, you don't think Stacey did it?"

He ignored her question. "Please tell me you haven't been back near the Charmers' house last night or this morning?"

"No, we haven't. We only got to the fence line last night and that was all."

He shook his head. "Please promise me you'll never do anything like that again. It was very silly. Risky, I should have said."

Elsa-May shook her head. "We don't promise anything. We just say we won't do it and that's enough."

"And we can't tell you we won't when there's a chance we might," Ettie added.

Elsa-May nodded in agreement with her sister and Detective Kelly grunted his disapproval.

"So, Detective Kelly, do you still think Stacey did it?" Elsa-May repeated her sister's unanswered question.

"My mind is open to all possibilities for the moment." He scratched the back of his neck and frowned. "I would like to know who that person was last night and why he was there in the house."

"I think it was the son," Elsa-May said. "It must've been. He might've wanted a keepsake from his father."

Kelly nodded. "That's very possible. Hopefully, we can find that out from the tire tracks. I'll pay him a visit this afternoon and see what he has to say. No point jumping to conclusions. We have to deal in the facts."

"I wasn't suggesting otherwise," Elsa-May said.

It was half an hour later before two white vans pulled up at the house and Detective Kelly set three evidence technicians to working on the tire tracks and then he sent more technicians into the house.

Ettie and Elsa-May watched from their window. "Ettie, you shouldn't have said I made you go with me last night."

Ettie knew that remark would've gotten under her sister's skin. "It doesn't matter." When her sister wasn't satisfied with that, she knew she was in trouble. "All right, I shouldn't have said it because you didn't force me to go with you."

"No, I didn't."

She turned slightly to face Elsa-May. "I was afraid to let you go alone. Do you want me to set things straight with Kelly about that?"

"He'll think we're mad."

"He already does, I'm sure."

The sisters laughed.

AFTER SOME TIME HAD PASSED, Kelly walked back to the ladies who were now at their front gate. "We were lucky it didn't rain last night and they parked in a good amount of dirt."

"Very good," Elsa-May said.

"And now they're taking fingerprints in the house. You didn't see if he was wearing gloves by chance, did you?"

"No, we didn't. I mean, I didn't. Did you notice that, Ettie?"

"I was too scared. I just saw a male running past and then he got into the car, turned it around and drove away. He was wearing a pullover, a jacket with a big loose hood on it. You know the ones?"

"I do. Anything else you remember?" asked Kelly.

Both ladies shook their heads.

"If it wasn't the son, it could've been someone who worked at the restaurant. The restaurant manager never got along with Greville. The one who lost his job, well, he was demoted when Greville was employed," Elsa-May said. "There's a word for employing relatives, but it escapes me at the moment."

"Nepotism," Kelly said. "It could have been a number of people. It might have been a criminal who knew the house was vacant. He could have no links to Charmers' death at all if he was an opportunist and read about it in the papers."

Elsa-May shrugged her shoulders. "Why rob a place that had already been robbed?"

"You don't read the papers, do you?"

Shaking her head, Elsa-May said, "No, not your papers. Only the Amish newspapers."

"I read newspapers and magazines when I'm waiting for Elsa-May at the doctor's."

Elsa-May frowned at her. "He's talking about something being in the paper in regard to the murder, Ettie."

"I know."

Kelly frowned and then said, "In the paper, it said nothing was taken. That might have led someone to believe there was actually something to take, but it wasn't found."

"Ah, I see," Ettie said.

"Hopefully whoever it was left behind a clue," Kelly said.

"We need to find out more about the sister. That's what I think," Ettie said.

Elsa-May nodded. "Yes. Why would Greville tell people that he was working for his cousin when it was really his sister-in-law?"

Ettie agreed, "It doesn't make sense."

Kelly raised up both hands. "Now let's call a halt to things right now. If you ladies keep putting yourselves in danger, sooner or later, you're going to find yourselves in a whole heap of trouble."

Ettie and Elsa-May exchanged glances. "We're in too deep to stop now," Ettie said.

Elsa-May hunched her shoulders. "No one would kill us."

"They might. Keeping out of jail is strong motivation and if they've killed once they won't need too much encouragement to do it again. This is my job and that's why I do what I do. I'm committed, but you two have nothing to gain by getting involved."

"We were asked to by Stacey in the first place," Ettie said.

"So what?" Kelly said.

Ettie nibbled on the end of a fingernail. She didn't fancy being murdered just because she was in the way of something. "If Stacey killed him and she was too scared to admit it straight up, that means there was no intruder, so who was that person in the house last night?"

Kelly smoothed a hand over his thinning hair. "I'm hoping that will be revealed if we find a fingerprint or two. All this talk is going around in circles and I'm a very busy man." Kelly stood. "Keep me informed if you see or hear of anything suspicious."

"Thanks for stopping by." Ettie rose to her feet.

When they had showed Kelly out, Elsa-May let Snowy back into the house. "I'll walk Snowy later. I'll wait until everyone leaves from next door."

Ettie looked out the window as she sat down on the chair pushed next to it. "I'll let you know when they go."

CHAPTER 16

IN THE MIDDLE of the afternoon, after Snowy's and Elsa-May's walk, Ettie saw a taxi pull into the driveway next door. "She's back, Elsa-May."

"Let's go see her."

"Okay."

Together, they walked over and saw Stacey pulling two bags of groceries out of her car.

"How did everything go, Stacey?" Elsa-May asked.

"They charged me and I got bail. My sister took me back to her place to freshen up and she also put up the bail money. That was good of her." Stacey sighed. "It was fifty thousand dollars' worth. I mean, where would I go? I don't know why they made the bail amount so high. I'm not about to leave the country and I even confessed. My lawyer thought that was a high amount—don't you?"

Ettie gasped. "That is a lot of money."

"Just a second. I have to put the groceries in the house and pay the driver."

Ettie and Elsa-May helped her by pulling out grocery

bags from the trunk. After Stacey paid the driver and he drove away, she swivelled around to face them. Her gaze dropped to the bags in their hands. "Just drop them by the door."

"We'll take them inside for you."

"No. It's okay. I'll do it."

Elsa-May and Ettie did as she asked and Ettie counted eight bags of groceries. "You've got a lawyer now?" Ettie asked.

"Yes. I'm using the one my sister found. She had to take out some kind of a loan to pay the bond. I'll have to pay her back the interest and what not, but you have to do what you have to do."

"Would you like to come over for lunch? Elsa-May's just made pumpkin soup and I've baked bread just now."

"The pumpkin came fresh out of our garden this very morning."

"That's kind of you, but no thank you. I just want to stay home and pretend to be a normal woman for one day." She sighed and her mouth turned down at the corners.

"Will you be all right going back into the house?"

"It's my home. Of course, I'll be all right. There's nothing to be scared of in there. The danger has passed, I'm sure of it. I don't think that man will come back."

Ettie and Elsa-May looked at one another. "So, there *was* a man who attacked Greville?"

Stacey shook her head as laughter escaped her lips. "That's right. I forgot I needn't carry on with all the lies to protect myself. There was no one else there that night."

It didn't seem like Kelly had told her about the man in

her house last night. "Didn't Kelly tell you that there was someone in your h..."

"It's all right, Ettie. Your detective friend told me someone was in the house flashing a light around. I'm pretty sure I know who it was. I can't tell you, but he's no one to worry about."

Elsa-May stepped forward and put a hand lightly on Stacey's shoulder. "If you need anything, just let us know."

"I'm fine." She gave them a little smile, and then turned toward her front door. When Stacey stepped on her door mat, she swung around. "Oh, you might be able to help me."

"What is it?" Ettie took a step forward thinking she'd changed her mind about them helping her inside with the groceries.

"Do you know of a good lawyer?"

"Um, I thought you said you had one?"

"I do, but I could change my mind. I don't know how good he is and I need a good one, an excellent one."

"We used to know one didn't we, Elsa-May? The one who wore the baseball cap. I can't remember his name, but we could find out."

"Yes, he was very good. Young, but good."

Stacey scowled. "Oh no. I couldn't use someone who wears a baseball cap."

"He didn't wear it in court," Elsa-May said. "He wore a nice suit and looked very respectable."

"Don't worry, I'll find my own." She unlocked her door. "Bye, ladies," she called out over her shoulder as she picked up two bags of groceries.

"Bye," the sisters said in unison.

Ettie and Elsa-May walked back to their house. "She seemed a little hostile," Ettie whispered.

"She's been through a lot with having to stay in jail and then going to court."

"There's worse to come for her," Ettie said. "There'll be a trial and everything, won't there?"

"I guess so, but she has confessed, so there might not be a trial as such." Elsa-May shrugged her shoulders. "I'm not certain about these things. She could get sentenced without a trial."

"She's cross with us over something. She wouldn't let us help her and she didn't want any of our pumpkin soup."

Elsa-May took a few more steps before she said, "She's just tired, Ettie, from spending the night locked up."

Ettie sighed. "Maybe."

CHAPTER 17

Later, over their second bowl of soup, the sisters' conversation once again turned to Greville's murder and Stacey. "Who's she protecting, Ettie?"

"I was just wondering the same thing. The estranged son, who killed his father in a rage, or the sister-in-law?"

"Greville's estranged sister-in-law, also his boss," Ettie corrected her sister.

"Formerly estranged but not anymore, it seems. Or could it be someone from his work?"

"Then we're in agreement she didn't do it?" Ettie asked.

"*Jah.* I don't think she did. Put it this way, I'm not convinced she did it."

"Me either. When she told us she killed him, she asked us to stop investigating, but why would we keep investigating once we learned she confessed? That was the part that didn't make sense to me."

Elsa-May's mouth opened wide. "*Nee,* it didn't. I hadn't noticed that until you mentioned it."

"Some things we don't know are, why had they disowned the son? And, also why was Stacey reluctant to get in touch with her sister?"

"She said they haven't always gotten along, so it could be just that. You know how some sisters are?"

Ettie slowly nodded. "Just like you and me."

Elsa-May fastened her blue eyes onto Ettie's dark ones. "What do you mean?"

"We don't always get along." Ettie giggled recalling their frequent disagreements.

"*Jah,* we do."

Ettie raised her eyebrows, surprised at Elsa-May. "Is that what you think?"

"We get along great. Otherwise, how could we have lived together for so long?"

"We do get along quite well most of the time," Ettie agreed and then gave another little giggle. "Anyway, that aside. Let's find out why the son was …"

"Forgotten?"

"Let's call it estranged. Disowned sounds awful."

Elsa-May stared at Ettie. "I didn't say disowned."

"I know you didn't. I was thinking it and was just about to say disowned and then changed my mind to say estranged."

"Oh, then why didn't you say so?"

Ettie's face screwed up. "I didn't think I'd need to."

"Okay, forget it." Elsa-May shook her head. "Where do we start from now?"

"Why don't we visit Evelyn, the sister?"

"But, Ettie, it wasn't a female who ran past us it was a male."

"Just because someone was in the house where someone was killed doesn't mean he was the murderer. And if it was Evelyn who killed Greville, she's not going to kill us in broad daylight. There's no danger. If she killed Greville, she had some reason of her own and it had probably been brewing for years."

Slowly, Elsa-May nodded. "When should we visit her?"

"I'd rather do it tomorrow, but we don't want to visit her and run into Stacey. We should see her right now because I don't think Stacey's going anywhere today."

"*Nee,* it looked to me like she was staying there all day. Do you have the sister's address?"

"Stacey gave it to us the other day."

"Grab it and let's go. I want to be home before dark. While we're there, we must learn all we can about Logan."

ELSA-MAY AND ETTIE stayed in the taxi when it stopped. "Is this it?" Ettie asked the driver.

From the front seat, a gruff voice replied, "This is the address you gave me."

Elsa-May tapped Ettie. "Let's go, Ettie."

Once Ettie paid the driver, she asked him, "Could you wait a few minutes for us?"

"I could, but I'll have to keep the meter running."

Ettie looked up at Elsa-May. "Go on."

"Yes, please wait. We might only be ten minutes."

"Okay. It's your money."

"Could you wait up the street a little?"

He frowned. "All right."

Ettie and Elsa-May got out of the car and looked at the

small house again. "I was expecting something a little grander since she owns lots of businesses. I thought she'd be wealthy."

"She might be."

Ettie looked at the peeling paint above the doorway. "It doesn't look like it."

"Shh, she'll hear you."

The two sisters walked through the front gate and knocked on the dark green front door. Ettie wondered if this might be the old family home where Stacey and Evelyn had grown up.

The door opened and Evelyn stood there in a dressing gown. "Oh, it's you two. I wasn't expecting visitors. I was having a little lie down."

"We're sorry to disturb you—"

Elsa-May interrupted Ettie, "We're worried about Stacey."

"That makes three of us." She stepped aside to allow them through. "Come in. Is Stacey all right?"

"She is. She's home, and she's resting."

"Ah, good. I've been dreadfully worried." She showed them through to a sunroom that overlooked a long and narrow garden.

The inside of the house was much grander than the outside. Ettie was admiring the flowers and would've loved to take a walk and have a further look at all the plants, but they were there about Stacey.

"Has Stacey said something to you to make you worried?" Evelyn asked.

"No" Elsa-May repositioned herself on the couch and

pulled a cushion from behind her back and placed it beside her. "She's said nothing much."

Evelyn shook her head. "Despite what she admitted to, she didn't kill Greville. She didn't tell me she did it. If she'd done it, she would've said so to me. What I think is that their no-good son did it and she's covering for him."

Elsa-May's eyes bugged open wide. "You think Logan killed his father?"

"I do. He was always after money. I told Stacey to be careful because if he was after his parents' money, Stacey's still in danger."

"Did they have a lot?"

Evelyn tilted her head and shrugged. "I have no idea about that."

Ettie wondered if that was why the son had come back that night—assuming it had been him—because he was looking for some kind of paperwork.

"I thought Logan did it as soon as I heard the dreadful news."

Elsa-May breathed out heavily. "Did you tell the police that?"

"No, I couldn't. Stacey would never talk to me again. I didn't tell the police what I thought. I have no proof anyway and they're always looking for proof, not hunches."

"But she could be in danger, if you're right about him," Elsa-May said.

"She asked me to keep out of things, so that's what I'm doing." Evelyn stared at Elsa-May. "Why don't you do the same?"

Ettie was surprised by Evelyn's attitude and guessed

she didn't know about the person in Stacey's house. "We're worried about her, that's all."

"I know. I am too, but she's old enough to make up her own mind how she wants to live her life. If she wants to cover for Logan, then it's up to her. I told her I'd abide by whatever decision she made. That's all an older sister can do. Now, can I offer you a cold drink?"

Ettie stood up convinced that Evelyn didn't really think Stacey was in danger because Logan had done it. "No thank you. We've got to keep moving."

"Yes." Elsa-May pushed herself to her feet. "We just wanted to see if there was anything we might be able to do to help Stacey."

"She's got a lawyer. He's the only one who can help her now. Unless … unless you'd like to say a little prayer for her?"

Ettie nodded. "We'll do that. We've already been doing that. Would you know how we can get in contact with Logan?"

"Goodness me, no. No one knows that. Not even his mother."

"Oh. I see."

The sister showed them to the door, and Ettie couldn't wait to leave. She hadn't even gotten a chance to compliment the woman on her lovely garden.

"What do you think about that, Ettie?"

"Weird, that's all I can say. She's not acting right. She's prepared to let her brother-in-law's killer go free and most *Englischers* want justice in this life."

"I agree, but she did make some valid points so I can see how she's thinking."

"If Stacey's in danger like she thinks, we should tell Kelly."

Elsa-May nodded. "Most definitely." When they reached the taxi, they had the driver take them directly to the police station.

AFTER THEY HAD WAITED an hour to see Detective Kelly, he finally called them into his office and they sat down in front of a grumpy-looking man. Ettie was sure his mood was sour because they weren't minding their own business instead of fussing over who killed Greville. "We think Stacey might be in danger."

He frowned more intensely, looking from one woman to the other. "From whom?"

Elsa-May took over. "Her son. It seems he might want his parents' money, and since they haven't helped him out, he's taking matters into his own hands. That's what Evelyn told us. She said she didn't know if they had a lot, but the way she was talking I'm wondering if they might have more than we think."

Slowly he nodded, but the ingrained frown lines on his brow didn't lessen. "You deliberately visited Evelyn to see what you could find out?"

"That's right, and maybe Stacey is protecting him not knowing, not realizing, that she could very well be next. That could've even been him at the house looking for her the other night, trying to kill her. He wouldn't have known she'd confessed to cover for him and was staying the night in jail." Ettie stared at Kelly, hoping he wouldn't be too angry with them, but from the thin line that seemed to have permanently replaced his mouth, she knew he was still upset.

"There's more." His gaze dropped to the desk and it was then that Ettie knew something more than the two of them had upset him.

"You've found out something else?" Elsa-May asked.

"I've been thrown quite a curve ball." He picked up a pen and tapped the end of it on his wooden desk. "You won't believe it and I will tell you since you're both heavily involved now."

"Yes?" Elsa-May asked, leaning forward eagerly while Ettie held her breath.

They continued to sit quietly in front of him as he used the pencil to scratch his head. He'd never done that before in their presence and Ettie was worried about him, but she had to exhale before she passed out.

The pencil fell from his hands and rolled onto the desk, then stopped. Kelly took his eyes off the pencil and looked up at them. "We routinely run prints as part of the autopsy and, funny thing is, Greville—or I should say, the man we found on the floor of your neighbor's house—was not Greville Charmers."

CHAPTER 18

"What?" Ettie yelped.

"It *was* Greville, we saw him for ourselves," Elsa-May said. "It most definitely was."

"Yes, no doubt about it. It was him and he was very much dead."

Kelly shook his head. "It wasn't. The deceased on your neighbor's floor was Kevin Garcier."

"No, we saw him. It was Greville lying there," Elsa-May repeated.

Kelly raised his hand to silence them. "Kevin Garcier was released on early parole from prison three weeks ago today."

"There must be some mistake."

Ettie shook her head, picturing Greville as he lay there lifeless on the floor. "Tell me again?"

"The man who was dead in your neighbor's house was not Greville Charmers."

"Yes, it was," Ettie said, taking a sidelong glance at her sister. "We saw him."

Elsa-May's face soured. "What does Stacey say about all this?"

"We don't know because we can't find her."

"She was at home today, before we left to visit her sister."

He pushed out his lips. "She wasn't home half an hour ago."

"Did you try her sister's place? We were just there, but she could've got there just after we left."

"I've had people out looking everywhere. She's not at the sister's house and her son hasn't seen her."

"Did you tell the son about this Kevin person?"

Kelly nodded. "I did. He said he doesn't know anyone of that name, but funny thing is we just found out Logan is on the visitors' log. Logan visited Kevin Garcier in jail twice in the past year. What's more, we couldn't find his name at first because he's not Logan Charmers, he's Logan Garcier."

"This is getting weirder. You mean, Greville wasn't Greville? And …"

Elsa-May stopped talking, so Ettie had to take over. "But we saw Greville dead and why does Logan have a different last name than he should?"

"I thought you two might be able to shed some light on the whole thing."

The sisters shook their heads.

"Well, I'll let you in on a little secret that explains a lot." Kelly smirked and the two sisters leaned toward him. "There was blood found on the victim's clothing, which belonged neither to the victim or Stacey."

"Greville's?" Ettie asked.

"The son's?" Elsa-May suggested.

"The blood we tested was a match for a sibling of the deceased, Kevin Garcier."

"A twin, an identical twin?" Ettie asked.

Kelly nodded once, and then shook his head. "Not exactly that, but a brother —maybe a fraternal twin—who looks strikingly similar. If they were identical twins, they would have identical blood markers and we might not have learned that there was a brother in the picture."

Elsa-May licked her lips. "Greville's brother, Kevin, gets out of prison, goes to see Greville and Greville kills him and then flees?"

Kelly raised his hands in the air. "It's a mystery all right. Do you see why we need to speak with Stacey? It's possible she knows all that happened. We also need to find out why Logan lied about visiting his uncle. And, his tire tracks matched the ones we found and that places him in the house with the flashlight. There's no point taking his fingerprints because he said he visited his folks so his prints would be inside the house."

"So, it was him with the flashlight inside the house?"

"He denies it still, but the tire tracks matched his. We've nothing to charge him on though." He picked up the pencil once more and tapped the table twice. "Why would he lie about it?"

"Well, it doesn't look good. It looks like he was trying to take something from their house. Why the different names?"

"They all used to be Garciers except Stacey and Greville changed their last names just before they moved to your street."

"I wonder why?" Elsa-May said.

"I don't know the answer." Kelly shook his head. "Sometimes folks do that when they're embarrassed to have a family member in prison."

Ettie said, "Maybe Stacey had no idea what was going on. She said she heard noises and sent Greville out to see who it was. I wonder if Greville didn't know it was his brother, and just thought it was an intruder."

Elsa-May gasped. "Does Stacey know she killed Kevin and not Greville?" Elsa-May asked.

"Oh dear." Ettie shook her head. "There was the funeral cremating the wrong man."

Kelly said. "That's right. And it leads us back to the question of who killed Kevin—was it Greville or was it Stacey? Stacey confessed to killing Greville and if he's still alive, it makes her arrest void from a legal viewpoint. Not that I'm an expert in the law, but—"

Ettie hit Elsa-May hard on the shoulder. "That's why he was wearing a suit, Elsa-May. Remember we kept wondering why he was in a suit rather than his pajamas?"

Elsa-May rubbed her shoulder. "Yes, but you didn't have to strike me so hard."

"Greville fled into the night in his pajamas. No, wait. The pajamas were in a heap in the room, so he would have changed quickly. That must be what happened." Ettie was pleased that the issue of the suit had been cleared up. "If Stacey didn't know what was going on at the start, she must've figured it out and that's why she's confessed to a crime she didn't commit. She's protecting Greville, not their son. Perhaps the brother—Kevin—and Logan were in it together to kill Greville, but the whole thing backfired."

Kelly said, "There could've been a plot to kill either brother, or no plot at all, just a series of unfortunate events. We can imagine whatever we'd like, but unless someone confesses or a reasonable explanation comes to the fore, we'll never know." Kelly leaned back and folded his arms across his chest.

"What was Kevin in prison for?" Elsa-May asked.

Kelly blew out a deep breath. "Writing bad checks and forging documents, as well as embezzlement."

"Not murder though, or anything violent?"

"No. I can tell you I was shocked when the prints got a match in the system and they didn't belong to Greville Charmers."

Ettie said, "That explains why the deceased had no poison in his system, because he wasn't Greville."

"Someone was poisoning Greville. It's my job to locate him and find out who was trying to kill him."

Elsa-May took off her knitting glasses. "Are fingerprints routinely taken when autopsies are done?"

Kelly nodded. "That's right, and for some reason I had them run the prints through the IAFIS database. I've always had something about Greville in the back of my mind. His name is familiar for some reason. Maybe it wasn't his name, just a feeling. Call it a gut instinct if you will."

Just as Kelly reached out to take up the pencil once again, Ettie leaned forward and managed to take hold of it just in time and she placed it down in front of her. "It's quite extraordinary. I wonder what Stacey will say about all this."

Kelly's lips down-turned at the corners. "We have to find her first."

"Do you think she's on the run?" Elsa-May asked.

"It's possible."

Ettie said, "I have a theory. Greville killed his brother, for whatever reason—I'm still not certain whether it was an accident or not—and then Greville, when no one believed the intruder story, told Stacey to confess to his murder to throw us off the track of what really happened that night. There was no danger at all of her going to prison because Greville was still alive. If she'd gotten off, all good, but if she'd been convicted, Greville could've reappeared."

Kelly slowly nodded. "That's a good reason for her sudden change of story."

"That could be true, because she begged us to help her find out who murdered Greville and then all of a sudden, she changed and said she did it," Elsa-May said.

"It was all very odd," Ettie agreed. "Surely she would've known it wasn't Greville lying there on the floor."

Kelly shook his head. "Who knows? Maybe not with all the confusion. Especially if they were look-alike brothers and she thought the other brother—Kevin—was locked up somewhere."

Ettie rubbed the back of her neck. "No, I think she knew at the start because she wanted Elsa-May to say she heard a car driving away."

"Oh, she did, did she?"

Ettie stared at Kelly not realizing they hadn't told him that. "We might've forgotten to mention that."

"That's a pretty important thing to keep to yourselves." Now the thin line of a mouth was back. "I'm disappointed in the both of you. Now it's all the more important that we find the missing Mrs. Charmers."

"She could be long gone by now," Elsa-May said.

"Hopefully not. She has to report weekly under the terms of her bail conditions, and we'll be waiting for her. If she doesn't make it or if she's gone out of state, she'll be in breach of bail."

"I don't think so," Elsa-May said. "Won't that arrest be overturned? As you said, she confessed to killing her husband, not his brother."

"It's gotten complicated, I'll admit that. We only have to hope she doesn't find out what we know before we can locate her. Now, the man you saw last night, did he have a large frame like Greville?" Kelly asked.

"No, he was much lighter and that's why we thought it might have been the son. Then again, it was dark and we were scared. He was moving fast. Are you thinking Greville might have borrowed the son's car?"

"I don't know, but Logan's next on my list to speak with—again." Kelly rose to his feet. "Let me know if you learn anything else. Are you heading home?"

"Yes. We are," Elsa-May said.

"I'll have someone drive you there."

Ettie smiled. "Thank you."

"No problem, and while they're there, they can see if Mrs. Charmers is back."

. . .

By the time Ettie and Elsa-May arrived home, it was nearly dark. The officers knocked on Stacey's door but the sisters knew Stacey wasn't home as there was no light coming from inside. They walked through their door and, while Elsa-May lit the gas lantern, Ettie walked to the couch and collapsed lifting up her feet and plopping them on top of her crocheted throw blanket. "Well, what do you think of all that?"

"Shocking and unbelievable. At least we have a clear idea of what happened. Greville killed his brother."

"No, we don't know that at all. That's what it looks like." Ettie sat up. "What if Stacey was in on it from the start?"

Elsa-May's eyebrows drew together. "What?"

"They lured the brother over there to kill him. Then because they keep to themselves and no one knows them, we didn't even know Greville had a look-alike brother, or a son. That's why they moved to this quiet location, they had it all planned out. If Kelly hadn't taken the prints to send to the ... whatever it was, then no one would've known it wasn't Greville who died. It was the perfect murder."

"*Nee*, it wasn't, Elsa-May, because everyone thinks Greville's dead. How can that be the perfect murder when Greville has to hide for the rest of his life?"

"When I said perfect, I meant ... Oh, don't bother." Elsa-May swiped a hand through the air.

"You know what, Elsa-May?"

"What?"

"That's why Greville acted aggressive and she acted like he was abusive. It was all a plot to kill the brother."

Elsa-May said, "Or, the other thing could be that it was an innocent mistake. The brother wanted to surprise them because he'd got out of prison early, they thought he was an intruder and killed him. They panicked and hid their tracks."

"Possibly, but why would they want to kill him?"

"Clean out your ears, Ettie. I said they accidently killed him and then panicked."

Ettie shook her head. "Sorry, I wasn't really listening."

Elsa-May huffed, looked disgusted with her and walked to the kitchen.

"Sorry," Ettie called after her. "I was thinking of something else while you were talking."

Elsa-May was gone for some time and came back with a plate of sandwiches for them. Ettie had hoped she was fixing them some food rather than sulking in the kitchen. Once Elsa-May sat back down, she said, "Don't you find that a little odd?"

Ettie took a sandwich. "What's that?"

"The whole thing. The name change, killing the brother, the son denying visiting the uncle and all of it." Elsa-May bit into her corned beef and pickle sandwich.

"Even Kelly is perplexed about the whole thing. I've never seen him looking so worried."

When they heard scratching on the back door, they realized they'd left Snowy outside and had locked the dog door. "I'll let him in. I can't think about any of it right now. If I think about something else, or don't think about anything at all, when I come back to it, I'll see it clearly." Ettie got off the couch and headed over to the back door.

Elsa-May put her half-eaten sandwich down, popped her glasses on and picked up her knitting. "Good for you."

When she unlatched the dog door, Snowy came bounding through giving Ettie quite a fright. He ran around sniffing the floor and then his sniffing led him to the corned beef sandwiches. Once Ettie sat down, she noticed Elsa-May had already eaten her share of the sandwiches. Ettie took some meat out of hers and gave it to Snowy. Then Ettie ate the rest of her share with Snowy's big dark eyes staring at her all the while.

CHAPTER 19

SATURDAY CAME and went with no sight or sound of Stacey or the detective. Ettie was pleased to put the whole thing out of her mind and help with the knitting. She couldn't knit all day, though, the way her sister could. Even with arthritis coming on Elsa-May was able to knit through the pain.

On Sunday, for the bi-monthly meeting, they were back to being collected by Ava and Jeremiah just like they had been before Aaron was born.

Ettie had been waiting by the window while Elsa-May was doing up her boot laces. "Here they are."

"I'm nearly finished."

Ettie shook her head. "If they can make it here on time and they have a *boppli,* I think you should be able to get ready in a timely manner."

Elsa-May looked up at Ettie. "Be kind. I'm getting older."

"You poor old thing. Would you like me to do up your laces for you?"

A smile spread across Elsa-May's face. *"Jah, denke."*

Ettie rolled her eyes, got off her chair and hurried over to tie her sister's shoelaces. "There. Now come on."

Elsa-May stood straight. "I'm ready."

"Finally." Ettie looked over at Elsa-May's sleeping dog. "Are we leaving Snowy in?"

"Jah. Just leave him in and we'll leave the dog door open."

When they got into the backseat of the buggy, they saw Aaron strapped into his seat fast asleep.

As Jeremiah turned the buggy around, he said, "Ava was saying something about scratching in your attic?"

"Jah, there was but it's gone now."

"It could be a racoon or something like that. I can come take a look this afternoon when I bring you home if you'd like?"

Elsa-May grinned. "Would you?"

"Of course. I'll climb up and see what I can see and block off any openings where it looks like something might be getting in."

"Denke, Jeremiah."

"Jah denke. That will put Elsa-May's mind to rest."

"There is something there, Ettie." Elsa-May leaned forward. "She doesn't believe there's been something scratching in the attic. She thinks it's all in my mind. Trouble is, she goes to sleep quickly while I wait up and hear the thing crawling around up there. I only hope it's a sweet woodlands creature and not horrid vermin."

Ava giggled. "Don't worry. Whatever it is, you don't want it in your house. Jeremiah will block off all the holes so it can't get in anymore."

"Denke. At least someone believes me." Elsa-May leaned back in her seat and then gave Ettie a sideways glance.

"I never said I didn't."

"Shh. The *boppli's* asleep," Elsa-May told Ettie.

When Jeremiah parked the buggy at the Grabers' house for the meeting, Ava walked to the house with the sisters. Aaron was still asleep as Ava cradled him in her arms. "I couldn't talk in front of Jeremiah but ..."

"What is it, Ava?" Elsa-May asked.

"I've been giving everything a lot of thought and what you need is to find someone who knew Greville. Did you know he's got a brother?"

"Jah, but how did you know?"

"Greville's son's Instagram. I got onto Logan's social media from the computer in the library and found out all kinds of things. And, did you know Greville and his son have different last names?"

"Jah, we only found that out recently," Ettie said.

"What else did you find out, Ava?"

"Well, I've already found Greville has an older brother and a younger one. The younger one's in college up north, from his Facebook. I did find there is an aunty who doesn't live too far from here."

Ettie stopped walking and they all stopped. "Greville has an aunty?"

"Jah, Greville does. Which means she's an aunt to all of them."

"That sounds more like it, Ettie. We can ask her some questions. I'd feel comfortable talking to a woman rather than a young man. What do you call not too far away, Ava?"

"Too far for a buggy, but a friend of mine will drive you. I've already asked if she'd take you." Ava looked over her shoulder at her husband, then turned back around. "You've met her before. She drove you somewhere a couple of years ago. Her name's Christina."

"Have we met her?" Elsa-May asked.

"Jah, I'm sure she drove you somewhere a couple of years back."

"We'll be happy for her to drive us if she doesn't mind," Elsa-May said.

"She insists she owes me a few favors and I'm taking this as one of them. She said she has tomorrow afternoon off and all day on Tuesday."

"Tomorrow!" The sisters chorused then looked at each other and laughed.

"'There's no time like the present,' our *vadder* used to say, and he'd say, 'Don't put off till tomorrow what you can do today.'" Elsa-May gave a sharp nod.

"While Jeremiah's up checking your roof today, I'll give you Christina's phone number to make your arrangements."

"This is very good of you, Ava."

"I would like to help more, but with this little one I'm limited these days." She gazed down at her baby with a smile just as they reached the door of the house.

THAT AFTERNOON, Ava fed Aaron in the kitchen of Ettie and Elsa-May's house while Jeremiah climbed into their attic.

Ettie and Elsa-May told Ava about the wrong man being buried and after Ava recovered from the shock, Ettie took up a pen and paper. "What's Christina's phone number?"

Ava gave the number she knew by heart.

"We would've told you earlier today about the wrong man being murdered, but there wasn't a lot of time."

"I understand. Call Christina soon, so she doesn't arrange something else for tomorrow."

"We will," Elsa-May said, "Just as soon as you leave."

"That sounds awful," Ettie told her sister.

"Ava knows what I mean, don't you? I'm not trying to hurry you off."

Ava laughed. "I know." She put her baby over her shoulder and burped him.

"How much do the brothers look alike?" Ettie asked Ava.

"They look very similar. Some of the photos were fairly old, but they had the same square jaw and close-set eyes."

"Hmm. Close enough for someone to think they were the same person?"

"I guess so. From a distance. And especially given he was dead."

Ettie nibbled on a fingernail thinking back to the man lying on the floor. She had wanted Elsa-May to check to see if he was still alive. In the end, she had been the one who felt for a pulse.

"Ettie, we had no reason to believe Greville was someone else, so we wouldn't have looked that closely."

"That's right, but Stacey would've known. And she said it was her husband—Greville—more than once."

"I hope you find something out from his aunt. Tell me as soon as you can, but not in front of Jeremiah."

They heard the back door open and Ettie and Elsa-May hurried out of the kitchen toward Jeremiah. "What did you find up there?"

"I couldn't see anything in the attic. It all looked pretty clean, no nest-building evidence or anything."

"That's good. We like a clean under-the-roof space."

"There were a couple of small gaps that I hit with a bit of filler and another slightly larger one that I blocked off with wood and then sealed the gaps around it."

"*Denke.*"

"You shouldn't have any more troubles. It might've been a small squirrel or a possum. Well, it could've been anything, but it won't be back inside."

Ettie made an excuse and pulled Jeremiah aside. "How are things with your carpenter's business?"

"So busy. I'm thinking of putting someone else on to help with the workload. I know Ava's missing me of an evening. Has she said anything?"

Ettie shook her head. "That's a great idea. You can't get the time back you know. Aaron will be bigger in no time. Enjoy your family while they're young."

He put his hand on Ettie's shoulder. "*Denke,* for the advise, Aunt Ettie. I've got someone I've been talking with and I'll see him tomorrow and tell him he's got the job. That will free me up to be home for dinner every night. I know Ava's been missing me, but I want to do the work while it's there."

Ettie smiled at him and nodded. "That will make all

the difference." It made her feel good to be able to help the young family.

When Elsa-May and Ettie's visitors left, the two sisters headed to the phone shanty and made their arrangements with Ava's friend. Then they walked home and settled down in the living room. Elsa-May dozed off while Ettie wrote some letters to old friends.

CHAPTER 20

As the two elderly sisters traveled in Christina's car the next day, Ettie leaned forward from the back seat where she sat with Ettie. "It was good of you to take us today, Christina."

"It's no problem. I wasn't doing much today. Ava said it would only take a couple of hours."

"It will. I only hope the woman we're coming to see is home."

Christina glanced at her in the rear-view mirror. "You didn't call her and find out?"

"No, we decided spontaneous might be better. We don't know her. We're hoping she'll talk to us."

Christina nodded and looked at the road ahead and Ettie didn't feel the need to tell her exactly what they were doing.

"Here we are," said Christina when she stopped the car in front of a small gray house with white shutters.

"You'll wait here?" Elsa-May asked Christina.

"I'll be right here." Christina turned off the engine and

picked up her cell phone while the sisters made their way out of the car.

As they walked to the front door, Ettie got nervous. "Will you do the talking?"

"Me?" Elsa-May asked. *"Nee,* you do it."

Ettie knocked on the door and as she waited she said a prayer for courage, as well as answers.

"I'm coming," they heard a woman call from within the house. A minute later, the door opened to reveal an elderly white-haired lady. "Yes?" she asked as she looked the sisters up and down.

Ettie opened her mouth to speak, but Elsa-May moved forward. "I hope you don't mind us visiting, but we knew your grandson, Greville."

"He wasn't my grandson."

"I mean, your ..."

Ettie chimed in, "Nephew."

"That's right he was my nephew. Did he owe you money, or promise you something?"

"No, no. That's not why we're here. Could we speak with you for a few moments?"

The woman frowned. "About Greville?"

"Yes."

"Come inside." She walked through to a small kitchen and the sisters followed. When she turned to face them, she asked, "Is here okay?"

"This is fine." Elsa-May sat herself down at the table.

"I made some iced tea this morning. Would you like some?"

Ettie sat as well. "That would be lovely, thank you."

The woman opened her fridge and pulled out a jug. "I put mint leaves in it to give it an extra zing."

"Good idea. We do that sometimes too. Oh, we didn't introduce ourselves. I'm Elsa-May and this is my sister, Ettie."

"I'm Valda."

"Nice to meet you."

"We lived next door to Greville and Stacey."

Valda made a face when Stacey's name was mentioned and then continued to pour three glasses of iced tea.

When she'd poured all three glasses, she sat down at the table with them. "Poor Greville. She was a dreadfully unstable woman."

"Stacey?"

"Yes. Stacey. You're not a friend of hers, are you?"

"We didn't know her that well." Ettie took a sip of tea.

"We never knew until recently that Greville had a brother who looked just like him."

Valda nodded. "The three brothers all are strikingly similar in looks. But all as different from each other as chalk and cheese, day and night. Do you know about Kevin?"

"Yes." Ettie wasn't sure what Valda meant, but figured they would get more information if she answered yes to that question.

Valda shook her head. "He's a bad seed. The three brothers were all so different from one another in personality but not in looks. Kevin hasn't even come to see me." Valda stared into her iced tea and shook her head. "I'm only glad their parents aren't alive to see how Kevin turned out."

She was talking about him in the present tense, so she didn't know he was dead.

"Now, what did you want to ask me?"

"Were you close with them? The three brothers?"

"No, not at all."

Elsa-May leaned forward. "Yet you expected Kevin to visit you?"

"Oh yes. He owes me money. That's the only reason. I'm not going to chase him for it. I'll leave it to his conscience."

"How long ago did he borrow the money?"

Valda took a sip of tea. "It would've been when he was a teenager."

"And did you get along with Stacey?"

She shook her head. "Kindly don't mention that woman's name in my house. I've never met anyone so odd. It always seemed to me like she was up to something. I never found out what."

"In what way?" Ettie asked.

"I can't put my finger on it. I just never liked her. Maybe that's what it was. Some people you like instantly and some, as soon as you meet them, you know you'll never get along with them."

"I guess that's true," Elsa-May said. "Did Greville say anything to you about Stacey?"

"Like what?"

"I don't know. Anything at all?"

She shook her head. "No. I didn't speak with them much after their wedding. It's very sad what happened to Greville."

After a few more questions it was clear to Ettie that

the woman wouldn't be able to help them. They drank the last of their tea and thanked Valda for her hospitality.

As ETTIE and Elsa-May walked from Valda's house to the car, Ettie whispered to Elsa-May, "When will someone tell everyone Kevin is the one that's dead and not Greville? It was clear Valda didn't have a clue."

"I thought she would have known by now."

"Me too. Kelly might not know of her existence."

"Could be."

"Perhaps we should tell him about Valda. You'd think if Ava found her easily enough then Kelly could find more relatives of Kevin and Greville."

"*Nee,* Ettie. They just need to inform the next of kin, that's all."

When they got back in the car, Christina turned to look at them in the backseat. "Are you all done?"

"Yes, thank you."

As the car pulled away from the curb, a car slowed down coming in the opposite direction. It was Kelly in the driver's seat, and he was staring at them. Elsa-May dug Ettie in the ribs. "It's Kelly."

Christina glanced in the rear-view mirror. "Do you want me to stop?"

"No, no." Elsa-May shook her head.

"No. Drive faster, please" Ettie said.

CHAPTER 21

When the elderly sisters had just put their evening meal on the table, there was a firm knock on the door and Snowy ran around acting crazy.

"Oh no." Ettie covered her mouth. "Kelly's here to tear strips off us."

"You keep the dinner warm in the oven and I'll put Snowy outside."

"Coming," Ettie yelled to the person at the front door that she guessed was Kelly. Once Snowy was outside the two ladies proceeded to the door. Ettie got there first and opened it. It was Kelly, of course, and he was glaring at them as expected.

"What were you two doing today?"

"You saw us, didn't you?" Elsa-May asked.

He folded his arms across his chest. "Why were you there?"

"To see what she knew about Greville and Kevin."

His eyebrows drew together. "What did you tell her about them?"

"Nothing. We didn't tell her that Greville was alive and Kevin was buried in his place and now Greville and Stacey are missing. Did you think she was hiding them there?"

He frowned. "No. She was informed the day we found out about the mix up with the brothers. She didn't know whether the both of you knew, so she was keeping it quiet. Then I had to tell her that both of you knew."

"Oh dear," Ettie said. "That makes me feel very bad for not telling her."

"I made your excuses for you, don't worry yourselves. What did she tell you?" Kelly asked, on his way to sit in the living room.

Elsa-May sat down. "We could ask you the same."

He chuckled and sat down heavily on one of their wooden chairs. "She didn't know anything and she talked about the brothers when they were boys. She hasn't seen any of them. She doesn't think much of Stacey. After Stacey and Greville married, she didn't have much to do with them."

"Valda was no help at all, then?"

He shook his head. "I see you have your own chauffeur now."

Elsa-May laughed. "That was a friend of a friend. Doing the other friend a favor."

"Ah." Kelly nodded.

"Stacey's back, Elsa-May." It was the next morning and Ettie had been drinking her hot tea by the window.

Elsa-May hurried over to look out. "What's she doing?"

"It's hard to see. She's driven so close to the house." They watched as she unlocked the door and then closed it.

"Should we go over and tell her the police are looking for her?" Ettie asked.

"She would know that, Ettie."

"Oh, here she comes."

Elsa-May peered out the window. "I can't see very well. Is she coming here?"

"Yes. She's past her car and heading down the driveway."

They went to the door and waited for her. A breathless Stacey hurried up their porch steps.

"I don't know if you know the latest?"

"What's that?" Elsa-May asked.

"Greville is not dead. It was his brother. He'd just got out of prison. Now, I don't know where Greville is. At least I'm not arrested."

"They're not blaming you for his brother's death?"

"Not now at least. My lawyer did some work and I'm no longer arrested. All my charges were dropped. I just have to hope they don't bring new ones against me." She wiped away a tear. "It's all been so stressful. I said goodbye to Greville, but it wasn't Greville. It was definitely his brother because of the DNA match."

"You don't know where Greville is?"

"As far as I knew, he died on my floor." She shrugged her shoulders. "Unless the authorities have gotten it wrong."

"So, Greville killed him, his own brother?"

"I don't know. I heard a scuffle. Then, when I got to the living room, a man was dead on the floor and I thought it was my Greville. Greville must've killed him and run away in fright. I'm sure he'll be back. At least I'm free now and to show my appreciation I'm going to bake a fruit cake for both of you. I just bought all the ingredients today."

Elsa-May shook her head. "There's no need to do that, Stacey, truly."

"I haven't baked for so long and now I feel the urge. It must be that taste of freedom." She took a deep breath. "I'll be back when I've baked it. I've bought all fresh ingredients." She turned around and hurried back down the steps.

"We don't need fruit cake," Ettie said under her breath. "It's nice of her to think of us at a time like this."

"It seems she has nervous energy. Baking a cake is probably good for her."

Ettie closed the door.

IT WAS two hours later when Stacey came back with a still-steaming cake on a plate. "I didn't know it would take so long. I thought it would be ready in half an hour, silly me, but the recipe said to bake it for an hour and twenty minutes. I hope it tastes all right. Would you like to try it?"

Ettie looked at the cake. It appeared a little dry and over-baked. "It looks tasty, but we've just had our lunch. Can we leave it for dessert, for after our evening meal?"

The smile left her face. "Oh. I thought you might try some now."

"We would but we have no room," Elsa-May said taking the tray from her.

Ettie asked, "Would you like to come in for coffee?"

"No, that's okay. I hope it tastes all right."

"Won't you stay?" Elsa-May asked.

"I'm tired after all the baking. I'll go home now."

"Okay. Is there anything we can do for you?" Ettie asked.

"Enjoy the fruit cake, that's all." Stacey turned and walked out of their house.

Elsa-May placed the cake tray on the stove and then put her hand over her stomach. "I feel awful, but I couldn't have fitted another thing in."

"Me either. Maybe I should've forced myself to eat some."

"Too late for that. We've already upset her."

Elsa-May looked down at the cake. "Should we call Kelly and tell him Stacey's back?"

"*Nee.* He'll figure things out and it doesn't seem like she's going anywhere with all this baking she's doing."

THE NEXT MORNING, Stacey knocked on Ettie and Elsa-May's door. When Ettie opened the door, Stacey smiled at her. "How did you like the cake?"

"Um, it was lovely." Ettie didn't like to lie. They hadn't even had a little taste, but the last thing she wanted to do was to hurt Stacey's feelings.

Elsa-May walked up behind Ettie. "It was truly tasty. We must get the recipe."

"Well, if you liked that I've got something else for you that I baked this morning."

Ettie chuckled. "It seems you've found a new hobby."

The smile left Stacey's face. "You didn't eat it did you?"

Elsa-May said, "We didn't. it looked too good for us to eat, so we've put it aside for visitors. Fruit cake can last for months in an airtight tin."

"We should eat it," Ettie mumbled.

"We will when we have visitors. Would you like to join us for some right now, Stacey?"

"Not right now. How about I come back with my other cake for morning tea?"

"Okay."

"I'll be back soon. Unless, you were going somewhere today?" Stacey's eyes widened as she looked from Ettie to Elsa-May."

"We're not going anywhere. You come back whenever you're ready," Elsa-May said.

WHEN SHE WAS down the steps and out the front gate Ettie looked at Elsa-May. "What are we going to do? I hope the next cake looks better than the last."

Elsa-May chuckled. "*Jah*, I hope so too."

Ettie grimaced. "What if this becomes a habit and she wants to bake for us all the time? And stops by every day?"

"Stop thinking the worst. If this cake looks as bad as the last I think I'll have a stomach ache."

"I'll be on a diet."

"I'll be on a diet, it makes more sense, and you take the stomach ache excuse."

Ettie shook her head. "It's no good. I think we'll have to try a piece. I see no way around it." Ettie left her sister alone, sat down on her couch and started going over everything that had happened since seeing Greville, or the man they had thought was Greville, on the floor of Stacey and Greville's house.

TWO HOURS LATER, Stacey was back. "Let's sit down in the kitchen before I show you my creation," Stacey suggested, as she held a tea towel covered tray in her hands.

Ettie nodded "Okay; we've only just made hot tea."

"Good."

When everyone was seated, Ettie started talking. "I know both you and Greville killed his brother."

"Why would you think that?"

"The pajamas. You lured him there to kill him with the idea of swapping the brothers' identities. But, something went wrong and you had no time to put Greville's pajamas on him. That's why they were tossed in the corner. You wanted it to look like an intruder killed him when actually it was you or Greville who did it."

"Is that right, Stacey?" Elsa-May asked when Stacey kept silent.

Stacey pulled off the tea towel and instead of their gaze falling onto a cake, it was a gun. Slowly and carefully, Stacey picked it up. "That's right, Ettie. Well, you're nearly right and now I'm going to kill you both."

"What are you doing?" Ettie asked.

Elsa-May cringed. "Why are you … why do you want to hurt us?"

"Because I thought you were on to me and now I know I was right." Stacey gave an evil cackle.

"You killed Greville? I mean, Kevin?" Elsa-May asked.

"You might as well tell us, Stacey, since you're going to kill us anyway."

"Greville was too stupid to come up with any plan. It was all me. I had this planned for a long time."

"But you asked for our help to find his killer," Elsa-May said.

"I had to. You're friends of that detective, so I made myself believable to you, so I'd appear that way to him. Get it?"

Elsa-May frowned. "If you kill us, how's that going to look to the detective?"

"I don't care. I'll be long gone." Stacey giggled. "Don't worry, I've got it all figured out. I'm going to make it look like there was a struggle at my house and the cops will think I've been abducted, most likely by the same people who killed the two of you. They won't think to check the airports and I'll make my escape with my son and Greville. Kevin knew the right people to change our identification documents and we've all got new names. Lucky he did all that before he was killed. My name is now officially Amanda Pringle. How about that?"

Elsa-May screwed up her nose. "I don't like it."

"I like it," Ettie said, earning a frown from Elsa-May. "Tell us how it all came about before you kill us, would you?"

Stacey's eyes sparkled. "I might as well. Kevin stole

money and put it in an overseas account under Greville's name. The plan was for us all to live abroad when Kevin got out of prison. The account had been opened in Greville's name and he was the one who was supposed to get it out, but he changed his mind about the whole thing. When I told him I wasn't happy, he said I was pressuring him to be crooked just like Kevin."

Elsa-May nodded. "That's why he was so unhappy all the time. He was under stress."

"What did he change his mind about?" Ettie asked.

"He changed his mind about going overseas and being involved with any dishonesty to do with the money. When he found he'd killed Kevin and not an intruder, he had no choice but to go overseas and live abroad. He wasn't happy about including Logan, but I wasn't going anywhere without Logan. Logan's not his biological son, but that's another story altogether. They never got along."

"How did Kevin come to be killed?"

"Kevin was released earlier than expected, and we all kept it quiet from Greville because of my new plan."

"Which was?" Elsa-May asked.

"Kevin was to come here and kill Greville, and then take his place."

"How could you kill your own husband?"

"As easy as I'm going to kill the two of you. I used to hunt with my father. This is just the same only you two will be easy targets. Sitting ducks. Anyway, I was bored with Greville. He left his good job to throw toppings on pizzas. Not only is there no skill involved, there's no money in it."

"What happened that night of the murder, Stacey?"

Elsa-May asked.

"All Greville knew was I told him there was someone in the house and he went to investigate. That's when Greville killed Kevin by accident. He probably figured whoever it was in the house was trying to kill him and he retaliated. When I turned on the light, I couldn't believe my eyes and neither could he. Greville had killed Kevin and not the other way around. I didn't know what to do and yes, I took out a pair of pajamas to dress Kevin in to make him look like Greville, but you two got to the house too fast and ruined everything."

"That's why you came up with the story about him wearing his suit under his chef's clothes?" Elsa-May asked.

"That's right."

"That was an ingenious plan. What were you planning on doing with the body?"

"My original plan was to bury Greville deep in the garden under a fish pond. Greville had already dug a large hole near the back fence. Then when things went wrong, I told Greville to run and we'd pretend Kevin was Greville to cover up the murder. He agreed."

"So you do love him after all?" Elsa-May asked.

"Oh no. I needed one of the brothers alive so I could recover the money. If Greville went to jail, who knows when I would get the money, if at all."

"So, where's Greville now?"

"I'm not finished yet." When she gave another evil laugh, Ettie noticed a slight gap in her front teeth that she'd never seen before because Stacey so rarely smiled. "Then, Greville said that when the dust settled we should leave the country. My original plan had to change quite drastically of course." She gave a deep sigh.

"So Greville, wherever he is, has no idea he was the one supposed to be killed that night?" Ettie asked.

"Correct, and all would've been well except for your detective friend and his stupid idea to run Kevin's fingerprints through the system." She pointed the gun at them with her arms straight. That and the DNA from the blood."

"Where's Greville now?"

Her eyebrows rose. "Waiting for me to join him. Now, no more questions."

Elsa-May raised her hand. "One more question before you kill us. Was there poison in the cake you baked us?"

"Yes. And I went to all that trouble baking it." She clicked the gun. "Goodbye."

"Just a moment. Why did you deny having children?" Ettie asked.

"I said, 'No more questions.'"

"Elsa-May had a last question and I didn't have my last one."

"Ettie, even at times like these you're jealous of me." Elsa-May's full cheeks pouted.

Ettie's mouth dropped open. "I've never been jealous. You had a turn, now I want mine."

"Stop!" Stacey yelled. "You're driving me crazy. What's your question, Ettie?"

"I forget now." Ettie bit her lip.

"She wants to know why you always said you never had any children."

Ettie frowned at Elsa-May for asking *her* question,

when she'd really been stalling.

"When I suddenly disappeared to leave the country, you would've known as little about me as possible. Now, it won't matter because I'm going to kill you two right now." She stood up walked over and held the gun at Ettie's head. "You never liked me, did you?" she whispered in Ettie's ear.

"I don't dislike anyone, but there was always something untrustworthy about you. I must admit, I thought Greville was the aggressive one."

Stacey cackled. "You're a brave woman to say that when I'm just about to snuff out your lights."

"You're about to shoot me anyway. Just make it quick." Ettie closed her eyes, said a prayer and reached for Elsa-May's hand. Then she felt Elsa-May's hand wrap tightly around hers.

Elsa-May said, "You don't have to kill us, Stacey."

"It's Amanda."

"You don't have to kill us, Amanda. We won't stop you from doing anything. We're just a couple of old ladies, and we did try to help you because you asked us to."

"If I leave you alive, you'll tell that detective friend of yours what I've told you and my plan will be ruined. You should've just eaten the cake," Stacey snapped. "Then it all would've been done. We're leaving this evening."

There was a sudden knock on the door and when Stacey turned her head, Elsa-May released Ettie's hand and put both hands under the table and overturned it, knocking Stacey to the floor and tipping Ettie and her chair over. The gun went off. Ettie closed her eyes, her ears ringing from the gunshot and her heart pounding so hard she couldn't hear anything else, and then she heard Kelly's voice.

"What's going on?" Kelly yelled. Ettie opened her eyes. Kelly was now pointing his gun at Stacey, and his gaze flicked to the gun on the floor. He carefully moved it aside with his foot. "Is everyone okay?"

"She was going to kill us," Elsa-May said. "With fruit cake, and the gun."

So frightened was Ettie, she couldn't find her voice to utter anything. Kelly grabbed Stacey just as she made a lunge for the gun, and somehow, he managed to place her in handcuffs while Elsa-May hurried to help Ettie to her feet. Elsa-May righted the chair, and Ettie sagged onto it.

With Stacey's hands cuffed behind her back, Kelly pulled out his phone and called for backup. "Are you both all right?" he asked when he'd ended the call.

"A little shaken, that's all," Elsa-May said.

"Mrs. Smith?"

Slowly, Ettie nodded. "I'm okay. I'll probably be bruised, that's all. She tried to poison us with fruit cake and then she came to shoot us. If we'd eaten that cake we'd be dead by now."

"Where is that cake?"

"We've got it in a tin," Elsa-May said.

He pursed his lips and nodded. "Don't touch it. I'll take care of it."

Detective Kelly took Stacey out to his car and waited for a squad car to pick her up. Ettie and Elsa-May watched out the window while she was read her rights. Then the paramedics Kelly had ordered came and checked the elderly ladies over. After the paramedics left,

Ettie and Elsa-May huddled together and looked out the window.

"What a dreadful end for our neighbors. That was close, Ettie. She would've shot us. And, what if we'd eaten that cake? We might've if it'd looked more appetizing. If she'd been a better cook we'd be dead."

"I know. She was so calculating and evil. I'm still shaking." Ettie put her hand out for Elsa-May to feel.

"You're so cold, Ettie."

"That's not nice."

"I mean, your hand is cold. It's freezing to the touch."

"Oh." Ettie put a hand to her face. "You're right, it is cold. Thank you for your quick thinking, Elsa-May. I thought my life was over."

Kelly came back inside and he sat down with them while two police officers recovered the shell from Stacey's gunshot in the kitchen and took photographs of the bullet hole in the ceiling.

"What did she tell you?" he asked.

"She organized all of it. Kevin was hiding money in some overseas account with Greville's name on it, and Greville and Stacey were supposed to fly over there and get it out. Greville changed his mind so Stacey plotted with Kevin to kill Greville. Anyway, Greville wasn't supposed to kill Kevin, it was supposed to go the other way around. I think Greville truly thought he was fending off an intruder. To save himself from going to prison, Greville told Stacey to pretend his brother was him, and tell everyone robbers had killed him. When you got closer to the truth, Detective Kelly, that's when she decided to change her story to self-defence."

Elsa-May added, "That's when Greville decided to go along with Stacey to get the brother's money. He was a murderer now and probably felt that he had no choice. It was either go along with what Stacey wanted or turn himself in for killing his brother."

Kelly shook his head. "I don't know why Stacey ran such a risk when she admitted to killing her husband. She should've stuck to her original story and left the whole thing as a mystery. She's nothing but a cold-blooded killer. She was in on the plan to kill her own husband, and then covered up the crime that went wrong."

"I think she knew the story wasn't ringing true with anyone. There was no intruder and no evidence of one," Elsa-May said. "She was just biding time so she could slip out of the country."

Kelly nodded. "She must've been sure she wouldn't go to jail. Now all we have to do is find Greville. He hasn't used his credit cards or accessed his bank accounts and his cell phone has been switched off. We can't trace him."

"I'd say the son was in on it with his mother. He was the one delivering the messages to his uncle, while Stacey stayed at home pretending to be a battered wife." Ettie nodded her head toward Stacey's house. "Try next door."

"What do you mean?" Kelly frowned.

"For Greville. It's my guess he never left. That's why he was able to communicate so well with Stacey. He's hiding there somewhere."

"Are you saying he was there when the evidence technicians were there?"

"Yes. I've no doubt he was there all the time."

"They would've seen him. We combed that place for

evidence."

"Ah, but did anyone look in the attic? You weren't looking for a missing person back then."

Kelly's eyes opened wide. "Wait right there."

Ettie and Elsa-May rushed to the window and watched Kelly as he stood at the bottom of the next door driveway until four squad cars arrived. The officers hurried out of the cars and surrounded Stacey and Greville's house.

"Oh, I don't want to look," said Elsa-May.

"I hope he comes out of this unharmed."

"Who? Greville or Detective Kelly?"

"Both."

Several minutes later, a handcuffed Greville was led outside by Detective Kelly.

Elsa-May slapped Ettie on her shoulder. "You were right, Ettie."

Ettie rubbed her shoulder. "I don't know why you're so surprised."

THE SISTERS WATCHED until every last police car left.

Ettie moved to sit down on her couch while Elsa-May sat in her usual chair. "It's the end of an era, Elsa-May."

"I know. How will you fill in your days now?"

Ettie frowned at her sister. "What?"

"I said, how—"

"I heard you, I just don't know what you mean."

"You spent nearly every waking moment looking out that window at the Charmers, studying their every move, that's all I meant."

"We'll get new neighbors. Normal ones, I hope."

Elsa-May chuckled. "Please don't stare at them."

"I won't. I don't know how you could say that. I was only watching the Charmers because they were acting oddly. You know me better than that."

"Let's not argue about it."

"Suits me fine. You just keep on with your knitting and leave me be. If I want to look out the window, I will. I'm more of an outdoors person anyway. I don't like to stay in the house all the livelong day like you do. I like the fresh air on my skin and the sun on my face."

"Whatever you say. We'll have to let Ava know what's happened."

"We will, but not when Jeremiah's around."

IT WAS a week later when Detective Kelly visited them.

"He admitted to the accidental death of his brother. He also admitted there was a plot to recover the money and how he wanted no part of it until he found he'd killed Kevin. Him being in the house the whole time explained why there were no calls in or out from his cell phone. He was smart enough not to use his phone when he was taking cover within the house. And, I can tell you he had no idea what Stacey or her son had planned."

"No of course he wouldn't have."

"So, what you're saying is, Greville was innocent of any crime except for the crime of covering up his brother's accidental murder?"

He faced Elsa-May. "Not exactly. He was just about to go overseas and get the brother's money. They had airline reservations in fake names, the three of them. Greville, Stacey, and Logan, the son."

"But, he didn't go through with it."

"We'll let the courts decide his fate. Now, Mrs. Smith, I've been wondering how you knew Greville was still in the house?"

"Elsa-May's grandson, who is also my grandnephew, went up into our attic to block off holes where a rodent might have been getting in. I started thinking that a person could hide under a roof—in an attic."

"Is that it?"

Ettie nodded. "That's all. Oh, that and the fact that Stacey kept bringing a lot of food to the house. I also think the son had been communicating with him and that's why Stacey's son went there that day. As you said, they couldn't call each other."

"What's become of Logan, the son?" Elsa-May asked.

Before the detective answered, Ettie said, "I wonder if Stacey told him about the death of his uncle during the funeral service?"

"No. It was right before the funeral because he seemed upset. We noticed he left early and that's not the sign of a son grieving for a father. But wait, they never got along."

"Elsa-May, that was just a ruse to throw people off. That's why they came here and told us the story of having no children. They thought they could just slip away unnoticed. The only thing that went wrong in Stacey's plan was that the wrong brother was killed."

"Well, if you two are quite convinced you know everything there's no need for me to be here."

"Are we right?" Elsa-May asked.

"Let's wind back a few minutes, shall we? You asked me about the son. He was quite happy to give us evidence against everyone for a lighter sentence. It seems what you've been told about the son never getting along with the parents and vice versa was partly true, just not completely true."

"What did he say?" Elsa-May said.

"Nothing that we didn't already know."

"All's well that ends well." Ettie smiled.

"Now, how about a cup of *kaffe?*"

Kelly nodded and a smile lit up his face. "I would love one right about now."

"And, some fruit cake to go with it?" Elsa-May asked cheekily.

The detective threw his head back in horror and wagged his finger at Elsa-May. Then the three of them laughed.

~

Thank you for reading Fear Thy Neighbor.

www.SamanthaPriceAuthor.com

THE NEXT BOOK IN THE SERIES

Book 19
Amish Winter Murder Mystery

Tragedy strikes again in the Amish community when Ebenezer Fuller is found behind his barn, murdered. Ettie Smith is convinced she knows the identity of the killer until she learns surprising facts about Ebenezer's past.

The more Ettie learns about him, the more things don't add up.

Hidden secrets, false identities, and a surprise visitor, all add up to a busy winter for Ettie Smith and her sister, Elsa-May.

ETTIE SMITH AMISH MYSTERIES

ALL SAMANTHA PRICE BOOK SERIES

Amish Maids Trilogy
A 3 book Amish romance series of novels featuring 5 friends finding love.

Amish Love Blooms
A 6 book Amish romance series of novels about four sisters and their cousins.

Amish Misfits
A series of 7 stand-alone books about people who have never fitted in.

The Amish Bonnet Sisters
To date there are 28 books in this continuing family saga. My most popular and best-selling series.

Amish Women of Pleasant Valley
An 8 book Amish romance series with the same characters. This has been one of my most popular series.

Ettie Smith Amish Mysteries
An ongoing cozy mystery series with octogenarian sleuths. Popular with lovers of mysteries such as Miss Marple or Murder She Wrote.

Amish Secret Widows' Society
A ten novella mystery/romance series - a prequel to the Ettie Smith Amish Mysteries.

Expectant Amish Widows
A stand-alone Amish romance series of 19 books.

Seven Amish Bachelors
A 7 book Amish Romance series following the Fuller brothers' journey to finding love.

Amish Foster Girls
A 4 book Amish romance series with the same characters who have been fostered to an Amish family.

Amish Brides
An Amish historical romance. 5 book series with the same characters who have arrived in America to start their new life.

Amish Romance Secrets
The first series I ever wrote. 6 novellas following the same characters.

Amish Christmas Books

Each year I write an Amish Christmas stand-alone romance novel.

Amish Twin Hearts
A 4 book Amish Romance featuring twins and their friends.

Amish Wedding Season
The second series I wrote. It has the same characters throughout the 5 books.

Amish Baby Collection
Sweet Amish Romance series of 6 stand-alone novellas.

Gretel Koch Jewel Thief
A clean 5 book suspense/mystery series about a jewel thief who has agreed to consult with the FBI.

Made in United States
North Haven, CT
09 July 2022